EMERGENCY VETS

by Betsy Marino

Dutton Children's Books New York

For Stevie, Spot, and Sarah

Copyright © 2001 by Betsy Marino
All rights reserved.

Published in the United States 2001 by Dutton Children's Books,
a division of Penguin Putnam Books for Young Readers
345 Hudson Street, New York, New York 10014
www.penguinputnam.com

Library of Congress Cataloging-in-Publication Data
Marino, Betsy.
Emergency vets/by Betsy Marino.—1st ed.
p. cm.
ISBN 0-525-46662-2
ISBN 0-525-46501-4 (pbk.)
1. Veterinary emergencies—Colorado—Denver—Anecdotes
2. Veterinarians—Colorado—Denver—Anecdotes. I. Title.
SF778.M37 2001
636.089'6025—dc21   00-065858

Designed by Carolyn T. Fucile

Printed in USA
First Edition
10 9 8 7 6 5 4 3 2 1

Discovery Communications, Inc.
John S. Hendricks, Founder, Chairman, and Chief Executive Officer
Judith A. McHale, President and Chief Operating Officer
Judy L. Harris, Senior Vice President, Consumer and Educational Products

Animal Planet
Clark Bunting II, Executive Vice President and General Manager
Carole Tomko, Vice President, Development

Discovery Publishing
Stephen Newstedt, Vice President
Rita Mullin, Editorial Director
Michael Hentges, Art Director
Mary Kalamaras, Senior Editor
Rick Ludwick, Managing Editor

Emergency Vets was inspired by Animal Planet™, because life is better with animals. Action, adventure, comedies, pet care, and animal movies are all better with animals everyday on the channel that's filled with everything you love on TV, but with an animal twist.

Animal Planet™ is a trademark of Discovery Communications, Inc.

Acknowledgments

I would like to thank Dr. Robert Taylor and all the staff at Alameda East, especially Dr. Holly Knor, Dr. Kevin Fitzgerald, Dr. Steve Petersen, Dr. Dan Steinheimer, Dr. Doug Santen, Carol Rosenfield, Ray Parham, Janelle Stubbings, Matt Kelly, Terry Shand, and Amy. Your dedication to your profession was a daily inspiration.

I would like to thank as well Animal Planet and the staff and crew of *Emergency Vets*, especially Jim Berger, Karen Weiser, and Janice Jensen.

Also, Bob and Sarah, who never tired of hearing about animal emergencies.

A special thanks to Morgan Taylor and to the animals she grew to love, and to the Roscoes and Moo Shus that touched everyone around them with their silent courage. Also to Marissa and Taylor (Rick) for sharing their story of Rasta.

The final thanks goes to a woman who has spent her life in service to birds, Katherine Hurlbutt, or Birdy.

Contents

1	Not Just Cleaning Cages Anymore	3
2	Making the Rounds	14
3	A Ferret Named Ferret	25
4	My First Emergency	35
5	Pat the Hyena	49
6	Hanging Out with Holly	57
7	A Visit to the Bird House	72
8	A Cold-Blooded Surgery	81

9	THE QUEEN OF ICU	90
10	BREATHING EASIER	98
11	A FLIGHT OF FANCY	106
12	PIG OF HONOR	116
13	A CASE FOR A DETECTIVE	124
14	A SAD PRIVILEGE	132
15	THE DO AT THE ZOO	138
16	LAST ROUNDS	144

EMERGENCY VETS

Chapter 1

Not Just Cleaning Cages Anymore

I'VE WANTED TO BE A VET ever since I was three and a half, when my dad brought Dixie home from the pound. Dixie's our dog. *My* dog, really, since it's just Dad and me. She's a mix of Pekingese and poodle. The small kind of poodle—she weighs only about fifteen pounds, so I get to take her almost anywhere. Only I won't be able to take her with me this summer. I'm going to Denver to stay with my uncle Bob, one of the best veterinarians in the world. He's not just a vet, though—he's a surgeon. And he doesn't have just any clinic. It's a twenty-four-hour animal emergency hospital, and I'm going to be interning there for July and half of August. I'll be working with him and five other vets. My dad arranged the whole thing.

. . .

When Dad told me last week, I couldn't believe it. He took me out to Applebee's, which is my favorite restaurant because it's right next door to the Humane Society. Sometimes before dinner we go and look at the animals that are up for adoption. That night Dad didn't want to go in to see the animals, and he acted all mysterious.

"A special dinner for a special young lady," he kept saying as we waited for our table.

"What's so special?" I asked. It wasn't that big a deal to be going out to dinner. We go out at least once a week.

"I'm not telling—yet," he said, and then he roughed up my hair. I hate it when he does that.

Anyway, when Dad finally gave me the news, I couldn't help screaming. I think the whole restaurant heard, because just about everybody turned around and looked at me.

"I can't believe it!" I said. "Me, in an animal hospital for the whole summer."

It was a dream come true, really.

Then Dad did the parent talk. You know the stuff parents have to say to kids. The how-to-behave-when-you're-in-another-person's-house talk. The pick-up-your-towels, say-please-and-thank-you, and never-talk-back kind of talk.

I groaned. "Dad, I'll do fine."

"Oh, I know you will, and Bob's going to be a great surrogate dad."

"I don't need a surrogate dad," I said as I reached over to rough up *his* hair.

Uncle Bob is Dad's brother, and he's really nice. He's married to my aunt Barbara, and they have two kids—Allison and Tommy. Allison's six and Tommy's just about four. It's going to be a lot of fun living with my cousins, since I've always been an only child.

After dinner I called my best friend, Sarah, who screamed even louder than I had.

"Denver?" she said, amazed. "When do you leave?"

"Next Tuesday."

"Tuesday?"

"Yeah, and I won't just be cleaning cages."

Last summer, Sarah and I spent a week volunteering at the Humane Society, and all we did was clean cages. Still, we had a great time. Sarah loves animals almost as much as I do. Next to Dad and Dixie, I'm going to miss Sarah the most.

"This time I'll be helping with real medical emergencies," I told her.

"Great," she said with a little frog in her throat. "But what am I going to do all summer?"

"Oh, don't worry, Sarah. It'll go by fast, and we can write to each other."

Sarah and I decided to write each other every night, even if it was just a paragraph. Kind of like a diary for each of us to read.

"What about me?" Dad asked when he heard of my plan to write Sarah so much.

"You? Won't I talk to you on the phone?" I said, suddenly feeling a little sad.

"Of course." He smiled. "We can talk as much as you like, if you like."

"I'd like."

Dad's going to be pretty busy himself this summer. He's an architect, and he's been chosen to submit a proposal for the new art museum here in Santa Rosa.

"We're going to have to talk a lot," he said. "I'm going to need your advice."

Dad always runs his ideas by me. He says I am a born architect. But I already know I'm a born veterinarian.

• • •

Tuesday comes before I know it. After a flight that is so bumpy I almost lose my dinner, I land in Denver. Since it is my first plane ride alone, the flight attendant has to wait with me at the gate until I meet Uncle Bob. I don't mind waiting with her. I'm just glad to be off the plane and away from the man I was sitting next to—a fat, sleeping guy who drooled the whole time.

Uncle Bob finds me pretty quickly. Even though I haven't seen him in over a year, I recognize him instantly. He has on a pin-striped shirt and a maroon bow tie. He looks so much like my dad. He's got a little less hair, but the same face.

"Megan," he says as he hugs me, "my gosh, you've grown a foot, I think."

I laugh. "Maybe a couple of inches."

"No," he says, "I'm sure it's a foot."

Uncle Bob is more serious than my dad. He always seems more businesslike to me. Maybe it's because Dad would never wear a bow tie.

We pick up my luggage from baggage claim and walk to Uncle Bob's green Jeep.

"Mind if we stop off at the hospital on our way home?" he asks as we put my bags into the trunk. "I have a patient I need to check on."

"Sure," I say. Why wait to get started?

• • •

When I walk into the hospital for the first time, home seems a world away. Uncle Bob shows me the exam rooms and the two operating rooms.

"They're empty now," he says, "but tomorrow they'll be filled with pets."

Then he brings me to the Intensive Care Unit. This is where the really sick animals stay so they can be monitored twenty-four hours a day, by a doctor and a vet tech. "Vet tech" is just a short way to say "veterinary technician." A vet tech is the doctor's right-hand person. Ray Gordon is on duty now. He's tall and is wearing blue scrubs with a stethoscope slung around his neck. I learn that he's been a vet tech for almost as many years as I've been alive—ten and a half.

"Ray, this is Megan," Uncle Bob says. "My niece, and our newest intern."

"Welcome, Megan," Ray says. "It's nice to meet you."

Ray and Uncle Bob talk as they look intently into one of the largest cages toward the back of the room. A very big gray-and-black dog is lying inside. I think it's a Great Dane. Uncle Bob shakes his head as he looks over the dog's chart.

"What's wrong with him?" I ask.

"He's had something called a stomach torsion, which

sometimes happens in larger breeds. It's when the stomach and often part of the intestines flip. We did surgery on him this afternoon, but he's not looking great. The next few hours are the most critical."

I don't even know the dog, but I feel sad and worried about him. I bend down and give the dog a little kiss on the forehead. The dog looks up at me with the saddest eyes I've ever seen, but at the same time I see his tail start to wag.

"Ohh," I say, "you're a cutie."

When he hears my voice, his tail starts to go even faster, and it makes a loud noise against the cage.

"You're getting him all excited," Uncle Bob says.

"What's his name?"

"Samson."

"Is Samson going to be all right?" I ask. I hadn't given it much thought before, but suddenly I start to think that life at Alameda East might not be too easy. Especially for someone like me, who gets attached to any animal after about ten seconds.

"He could pull through just fine." Uncle Bob taps me on the head and kind of roughs up my hair the way Dad does. This time I don't mind, 'cause it makes me feel a little like I'm at home.

• • •

Uncle Bob finishes off the tour in the back kennel area, where the healthy animals stay. There are at least fifty cages here, all housing some sort of pet. I see furry cat tails and squealing pups, and even a green parrot in a large iron cage.

"Her name is Happy," Uncle Bob tells me. "I don't know why, though. She always seems mad about something or other."

"Does she talk?"

"Only to Janelle," he says.

"Who's Janelle?"

"Janelle's our head vet tech. She and I work together a lot."

Aside from Happy, who's a permanent resident, most of the animals are here for boarding. But I notice four or five cages with signs that say BLOOD DONOR. One sign says STRAY.

"What's a blood donor?" I ask.

"Blood donors are animals that belong to the hospital and are used to give blood to other cats and dogs that might need it."

"You mean they have no home?"

"Well, Megan, this is their home for now. After a year, we find them real homes with families."

"What about this one?" I ask, pointing to the cage marked STRAY.

"That one doesn't have a home. Or he might—we just don't know where it is yet. He was brought in by a Good Samaritan who found him on the highway. He had no tags."

The stray is a small, Lassie kind of dog.

"Does he have a name?" I ask.

"We've been calling him Bingo."

I stick my hand through the bars, and Bingo comes forward. He sniffs for a minute and then licks me.

"He's nice," I say.

On the way home, Uncle Bob tells me that every month several strays are brought into the hospital. Some are perfectly healthy like Bingo. Others need surgery or medicine or both.

"Can't they just go to the Humane Society?"

"Many of them can," Uncle Bob tells me, "but a lot of the shelters aren't equipped to deal with animals that need medical attention."

"So they come here," I say.

"Well, we help as many as we can, but unfortunately we can't help them all," Uncle Bob says with a sigh.

I can't imagine having to turn away an animal, but I

know it costs money to take care of them. I wonder if I'm too much of a softie to be a vet.

When we get to the house, Allison and Tommy are standing in the driveway holding up a sign that says WIL COME TO COLORADO. They're wearing pajamas.

"Megan, I just had to let them stay up to see you," Aunt Barbara says as she gives me a big hug. "They've been hounding me all day. 'When is she coming? Is she almost here? Is it Megan time?'"

I laugh. It feels good to be wanted so much.

"I like your sign," I tell them.

"We made it ourselves," Allison says.

After Allison and Tommy are put to bed, Aunt Barbara shows me to my room.

"The guest room," she says. "Though you're not really a guest—you're family."

"Thank you."

"Why don't you get settled, then come down and I'll give you a little supper."

I unpack and throw on some sweatpants. Then I go down to the kitchen, where Aunt Barbara has some chicken cutlets and mashed potatoes waiting for me. I think in all my excitement over seeing the hospital, I'd forgotten about food. I eat like I've never eaten before.

"You are hungry, aren't you," Aunt Barbara comments. "And a little tired, I bet."

"I don't feel that tired. I'm too excited about being here."

After I eat, I call Dad. He wants to know everything, even what I ate on the plane.

"Dad, I can't remember that far back. All I can remember about today is the hospital. And I know one thing."

"Yeah?" he asks. "What's that?"

"It's going to be different from working at the Humane Society. A *lot* different."

Chapter 2

Making the Rounds

THE NEXT MORNING, the alarm goes off at six o'clock, which for me is really five because it's an hour earlier in California. Uncle Bob warned me that most mornings we'd need to be in the hospital by seven-thirty for something called rounds. When I get downstairs, I can tell that getting up early is the thing to do around here. Everyone is already dressed and sitting down to breakfast. Things seem a little chaotic. My cousin Tommy is throwing Cheerios at Allison. Aunt Barbara has run out of milk, so we all have dry Cheerios and orange juice with Canadian bacon on the side. I can tell I'm going to like it here.

"My mom is big into Canadian bacon," Allison tells me. "Sometimes she makes us eat it on the way to the movies before we have popcorn. She says it balances out the popcorn or something. She's a little weird."

Making the Rounds

I laugh and look up at Aunt Barbara. She looks a little frazzled as she pours Tommy more juice, but I can tell she's a really good mom. She's also very beautiful, with dark eyes and hair. She looks a little like a movie star to me. She has a bit of an Italian accent because her mother was from Italy, somewhere around Naples. Even though she grew up in New Jersey, they spoke only Italian in the house.

Aunt Barbara, Tommy, and Allison wish me well from the front door as Uncle Bob and I climb into his Jeep and head off to the hospital. I can't believe I'm here in Denver, Colorado, so far away from the only place I've ever lived. Now that it's daylight, I notice how different the land looks here. I can see for miles and miles because there are fewer trees. The sky is clear and much bigger than the sky I see from our back porch in Santa Rosa. Uncle Bob points out a few sights on the way. He shows me a mountain called Pikes Peak. I'm surprised to see snow on the top even in July. I wonder if I'll get to see one of those peaks close up. After all, we can't work *all* the time.

"Here we are," Uncle Bob says, interrupting my thoughts, and like a dream, the day begins.

First comes rounds, when all the doctors stand together in the Intensive Care Unit and discuss each patient. It's a chance for the doctors who were on duty the night before to let the new doctors coming on know what's happening. It's also a time for the doctors to come up with solutions for each other's patients. Their chatter is confusing, because the language they use with each other is pretty technical, and there are so many animals with so many different problems it's hard to keep track.

After rounds, Uncle Bob immediately heads toward Samson's cage. He opens the latch and smiles as he pats the dog's head. I follow him.

"How's he doing?" I ask.

"He looks better. His incision is a little infected," he says, pointing to a line across the dog's stomach that looks red and painful. "But that's no big deal."

Uncle Bob turns to a woman standing behind him. She is wearing operating scrubs with a pattern of little cats and dogs. "Let's give him some IV antibiotic," he tells her.

Uncle Bob introduces me to everyone, and that's even more confusing than rounds.

There are six doctors on staff at Alameda:

1) Dr. Robert Taylor: Also known as Uncle Bob. He's the surgeon extraordinaire.

2) Dr. Steve Petersen: He's the second surgeon here

at Alameda, though he looks like he belongs in California. Hollywood, California. He's a cross between George Clooney and Leonardo DiCaprio. *Sarah would die right now* is all I can think when Steve Petersen winks at me.

3) Dr. Holly Knor: She seems too young to be a vet. With long blond hair pulled back in a ponytail, she looks like some of the kids back home at Teller High. "You can call me Holly," she says. "I can tell we're going to be friends."

4) Dr. Kevin Fitzgerald: The exotic-animal specialist here at Alameda. That means he gets to see not only dogs and cats but also snakes and lizards and ferrets and hamsters and sometimes even birds. He's seems to be three feet taller than me, and he's got thick gray hair and a funny mustache. He's also a comedian. Uncle Bob says Dr. Fitzgerald does a stand-up act downtown somewhere in Denver. I'd love to go see it!

5) Dr. Doug Santen: He has curly brown hair and a mustache that looks like it tickles. He's been at the hospital almost as long as Uncle Bob, and he seems like he's serious and cares a lot.

6) Dr. Dan Steinheimer: He has the funniest mustache of all. I think it might even tickle other people if they walked close enough to him. He's also got really long hair

that's tied back in a ponytail, and a really warm smile. He's the doctor of radiology, which is a fancy word for X-rays. Everyone calls him Dr. Dan.

There are also about ten vet techs—each doctor has a vet tech assigned to him or her. The others are assigned to different sections of the hospital, such as the Intensive Care Unit. The one in the dogs-and-cats scrubs is assigned to Uncle Bob.

"This is Janelle," Uncle Bob says.

"Oh. You're the one Happy talks to," I say.

"Yes." She laughs. "But I'm not so sure that's a good thing."

Uncle Bob puts me in Janelle's care for the first part of the day. She's been working with him for almost fifteen years. She knows about as much as anyone could about animals. The first thing she tells me is to keep my hands out of the cages, especially in Intensive Care.

"These animals are the sickest," she explains, "and what are you like when you're sick—grumpy or glad?"

"Definitely grumpy."

"Exactly. Intensive Care animals are the grumpiest, so never stick your hands in the cages, okay?"

"Do you think I'll see an emergency today?" I ask her.

"Well, we always hope not, but inevitably they come."

Suddenly I feel stupid for hoping to see an emergency. It's not like I want an animal to get hurt, but I think it would be kind of cool to see Uncle Bob working in surgery.

Janelle asks, "How long are you here?"

"Six weeks."

"Don't worry, you'll see plenty of emergencies."

I wince, but Janelle doesn't notice. She says, "Now let's go see that bird."

Happy is perched on a metal twig in the middle of her cage.

"Janelle, get out of town," Happy squawks. "Janelle, get out of town."

"See what I mean?" she says. "She's not very nice."

I laugh and walk up to Happy's cage. "I'm Megan. M-E-G-A-N," I say very slowly.

"Janelle, get out of town," she answers.

Janelle takes me around and introduces me to everybody else. She shows me the lab, where a vet tech named Amy heads up a team of five or six lab technicians. "This is where we test an animal's blood," Janelle tells me. I am fascinated by the lab. Dozens of microscopes fill a countertop that extends almost the length of the hospital. It reminds me of science class with Mr. Moore. It's kind of exciting to see people using a microscope in a real job.

After the lab, Janelle takes me to a treatment area in the back. This is where animals have their bandages replaced, nails clipped, and shots given. Sometimes it's where an emergency case comes first. Janelle asks Dr. Knor if I can shadow her for a while, and I follow a number of her cases. First, there's Penny, a four-month-old golden retriever that needs a booster shot. Then Sassy, a small tabby cat that needs some sort of kidney treatment. My favorite patient is Duby, a black Lab. Duby is a companion to a woman named Margaret who has arthritis. According to Margaret, Duby's very talented.

"She actually helps me do the laundry."

"The laundry?" I'm intrigued.

"Yes, she pulls the clothes out of the dryer. I can't bend down because my hips are bad."

Duby is in for an eye infection. I watch as Dr. Knor puts green drops in Duby's eyes and then inserts a tab of brown paper in each. She explains that the tear production in Duby's left eye is a little low. We turn the lights off, and Dr. Knor shines a special black light into Duby's eyes.

"Megan," she says, "right now I'm looking for ulcers. I can see a small one right over here in the left upper corner. Can you see it?"

I look into Duby's left eye and I see what looks like a clump of mucus that has been tinted green from the drops.

"I see it! I see it!" I say excitedly.

After Duby and Margaret leave, Holly tells me that these sorts of abrasions or ulcers are pretty common and that certain dogs get them more than others. "Like pugs and Pekingese and other breeds with bulging eyes," she says.

When she says "Pekingese," I start to get a little feeling in my stomach like I'm homesick. "I have a dog that's half Pekingese," I tell her.

"Oh yeah? What's her name?"

"Her name's Dixie, and I really miss her."

I think Holly can tell that I'm feeling sad, because she grabs my shoulder and says, "I had a dog named Dixie, too, when I was your age. Now I have two dogs. Would you like to meet them?"

"Meet them? Are they here?"

"Sure they're here. It's one of the perks of being a vet—you're allowed to bring your dog to work."

Dr. Knor's dogs aren't at all what I'd expected. For some reason, I pictured her with a Toto type of dog—the small cairn terrier that Dorothy carried throughout *The*

Wizard of Oz. Instead I'm met by an animal that looks like a small bear. "This is Kane," she says. "He's an Alaskan malamute."

"And this," she says, pointing to a rather old-looking black dog, "is Kingsley." Kingsley has a gray beard and eyes that have filmed over.

"Kingsley's a working dog," she says. "He has a pretty important job."

"A job?"

"Yes, Kingsley works at the Children's Hospital, visiting sick children. Maybe you can come with him sometime."

"I'd like that," I say. "I'd like that very much."

For the next few hours I stay with Dr. Knor in Treatment and watch her clip four sets of nails, including the nails of a 140-pound Newfoundland, whose name is Klinger. Klinger is nine months old and very energetic. He reminds me a little of the *Winnie-the-Pooh* character Tigger. I half expect him to start bouncing off the walls. Dr. Knor has trouble keeping him still. His thick black paws flail as he attempts to escape.

"Megan, maybe if you just grabbed the top of his shoulder and pushed his foot down, I could grab it and start clipping."

"Sure," I say, trying to sound casual, because I'm finding it hard to believe I am actually helping Dr. Knor with a procedure.

"Klinger hates to get his nails cut."

"That makes two of us," I tell her. I hate it so much that up until last year Dad had to sneak in at night and cut my nails while I was asleep.

"I have to finish up some paperwork over lunch. Why don't you just wander around and get familiar with the place," she suggests.

For a few minutes after Dr. Knor leaves, I stand around in Treatment, watching some vet techs replace a bandage on a Saint Bernard. I feel a little lonely and wish I had something to do. Everyone around me seems to know what to do and is doing it. I decide to go upstairs to the kitchen and eat the tuna-fish sandwich Aunt Barbara packed for me. Then I'll wander around like Dr. Knor suggested. Maybe with a full stomach I'll feel different. Less stupid, I hope.

The hospital isn't exactly pretty, and a lot of the rooms look alike. Metal cages and equipment adorn the ICU, Treatment, and X-ray rooms. Carole, the front receptionist, makes it easy for me.

"We've painted each room a different color. You can use that as a guide."

I walk around and see that Treatment is royal blue,

Intensive Care is purple, and X-ray is light blue. The kennels are yellow. I think I'm in a yellow mood, so I head back to where the little friend I made last night sits ready to talk to me. No, it's not the parrot.

"Hi, Bingo," I say, sticking my hand in the cage. Then I remember what Janelle said and pull my hand back. Bingo whimpers, so I decide to unlock the latch and open the door a little. I'm afraid I might get in trouble, but at the Humane Society I was allowed to open the cages. I had to—you can't clean a cage with the door closed. Besides, Bingo already licked my hand through the cage last night, so I know he's nice.

As soon as I get the door open, Bingo leaps into my arms. He wags his tail and covers me with kisses. "Hey Bingo, hey Bingo," I say over and over, grinning like crazy. Finally I feel like I have something to do.

Chapter 3

A Ferret Named Ferret

AFTER LUNCH, I FOLLOW Dr. Kevin Fitzgerald around. He's another one who tells me to call him by his first name right away.

"Or Fitz," he says. "Either one will work."

I like him right away. "True or false?" he says. "Cockroaches have four hundred thousand babies each year."

"False," I answer, because that seems impossible.

"True," he says. "Aren't they amazing?"

Fitz shows me his appointment book.

"Let's see if we have any exotics scheduled." He pauses. "We have a ferret named Ferret coming in. That's a pretty original name."

"At least it's not a dog named Dog," I say.

Ferret comes in with a girl around Allison's age. She

holds him on her shoulder, and as soon as he sees Dr. Fitz, he buries his head in the girl's hair.

"Oh, don't be afraid," Dr. Fitz says to the ferret. Then he turns to the girl. "Did you name the ferret? Or was it you?" he says to the girl's mom.

The mom and I laugh. And the girl proudly takes credit. "It was me, it was me."

The mom tells Kevin that Ferret isn't eating and for the last few days has been throwing up.

"The problem with these guys," Kevin tells them, "is they can't tell us where it hurts, so sometimes that makes it more of a challenge to diagnose."

Kevin feels the ferret's belly. "It does feel a little enlarged, and I think I feel something a bit hard."

He tells the girl that he'd like her ferret to stay with him for the afternoon. She looks sad. Dr. Fitz bends down so he is not so tall anymore. "See this girl?" he says, pointing to me. "This is Megan, and she's going to be with me all afternoon. Do you know what that means?"

"What?" the girl answers.

"That means she's going to be with your ferret all afternoon, right, Megan?"

"Right."

"And Megan loves ferrets, don't you?"

"I do," I say, and see that the girl is looking up at me now. She's beginning to smile.

"What's your name?" I ask her.

"Girl," she says, and starts to laugh.

"Well, girl named Girl, I'm going to take good care of ferret named Ferret, okay?"

"Okay."

"I'm going to take a blood test and see if Ferret has an infection," Dr. Fitz tells her. "Then I'd like to get some pictures of his belly. Would that be okay?"

The girl nods and walks out with her mother. Kevin motions for me to follow him. "Come on, Megan, I think you're about ready to draw some blood."

"What?" I say.

"I'm kidding." I watch in awe as he takes a needle, sticks it into a patch of fur, and comes out with a vial of blood.

"How do you find the vein?" I ask.

"Practice," he says. "And a little luck."

Kevin gives me the vial and asks me to bring it to the lab. I can't believe I'm actually holding an animal's blood. I don't even feel faint or anything. Last year at the Humane Society, Sarah had to sit down once and take deep breaths because a kitten's paw had been caught in the latch of the cage and was bleeding. I guess it takes a lot to make me queasy.

While Ferret is in X-ray, a dog named Schatzie comes in. Schatzie is a miniature pinscher, a tiny version of a Doberman pinscher. That's okay with me, because sometimes the big version scares me. Schatzie has nothing physically wrong with her. No ulcer in the eye, no eating problem, and she doesn't need her vaccine. No, Schatzie has an altogether different problem. She barks. And Schatzie's owner, an executive for an airline company, is beside herself.

"She's barking all the time," she says.

"A dog's got to do what a dog's got to do," Fitz jokes.

"Yeah, but the co-op board in my building is going to do what they've got to do and evict me if I don't get this dog to shut up."

"Well, tell me a little about what happens. Does she really bark all the time? Even when you are home?"

"No, only when I'm at work."

"And how long are you at work?"

"Well, I leave around seven and I get home after seven. Sometimes even eight."

"That's a long day. Where do you leave Schatzie during that time?"

"I had been giving her the run of the apartment, but

since the neighbors have complained, I've been putting her in a crate and leaving her in my bedroom with the door closed."

"No wonder she's barking," says Kevin. "If you locked me in a crate in your bedroom with the door closed, I might be barking, too."

Schatzie's owner smiles, and Dr. Fitz sits down next to her. "Let's see if we can come up with some solutions," he says. "It sounds like your dog just doesn't want to be alone."

Fitz recommends a doggie psychologist who might be able to help Schatzie with her separation anxiety. I think I know about separation anxiety. I got it real bad after my mom died in a car accident. Sometimes I still get that homesick feeling, even when I'm in my own bed.

Fitz and I talk about it after Schatzie and her owner leave. Fitz knows about separation himself. He was in an orphanage for about six years when he was a kid. A boys' home somewhere in north Denver. "It makes you strong," he says, "when you get through something you can't control."

The two of us go upstairs to the soda machine, and Fitz treats me to a Coke. We spend some time talking about Schatzie. Fitz thinks that the owner got the wrong dog for her lifestyle.

"That particular breed needs a lot of attention and can't tolerate that much alone time," he says.

A part of me wishes I could save Schatzie from her plight of living out her days crated in the bedroom, but Fritz says that would be interfering.

"Part of learning to be a vet," he says, "is letting other people take care of their pets even if we don't agree with how they do it."

I think about this for a few minutes. Isn't it cruel to get a dog only to leave her crated up all day? But then I think of Bingo. He's crated day and night. And so was every dog at the Humane Society. I guess Schatzie is a little better off, because at least she has an owner.

When Fitz and I get downstairs, Dr. Dan is in Treatment, holding up Ferret's X-rays. A crowd of technicians is gathered around him, looking at a spot on the film.

"You don't need to wait for the blood work on this one," he says over his shoulder to Fitz. "The mystery is solved. This little guy swallowed some sort of toy."

Dr. Dan and Fitz walk back to the X-ray reading room and put the films on the light box. Sure enough, there is a small object in Ferret's abdomen.

"It looks like a hook," I say.

"It sure does," Dr. Dan says. "But it's soft. Definitely not metal. Too thick to be a real hook, I think."

I'm amazed at how clear the image is. I've only seen a few X-rays in my life, and never any that I could actually spot something on.

"How do you get it out?" I ask.

"That's a good question, Megan," Dr. Dan says. "It's a lot easier to get it in than to get it out."

Dr. Dan explains that they have a few options. "We can wait and see if it passes on its own. Though this guy's been having signs for almost a week, so I don't think that's a good option. We can remove it surgically by cutting into the ferret's abdomen. Or we can try something called an endoscopy, where we try to retrieve the object by going down his throat with a special instrument."

Dr. Dan and Fitz discuss the case with Uncle Bob, and after getting the owner's permission, they all decide to do the endoscopy.

"This way we don't have to cut the ferret open," Uncle Bob tells me. "We always want to start with the least invasive procedure."

Uncle Bob will be performing the endoscopy.

"It's going to take a little while, Megan," he tells me. "Aunt Barbara can come and pick you up. You must be tired by now. It's been a long day for you."

I look up at the clock and see that it's five-thirty.

I'm amazed at how fast the day has gone and even more amazed that I don't want it to end.

"Can I stay, Uncle Bob?" I ask. "I told the girl I'd stay with her ferret all afternoon."

Uncle Bob smiles. "Of course you can stay."

The endoscopy takes a little over an hour. First Ferret is given an anesthetic, which puts him to sleep for the procedure. Then he's brought into a small room with a long table. There's equipment all around on movable carts. It reminds me of the audiovisual room at school. It looks like a TV and VCR with a hose attached. The hose is a camera that is slipped down Ferret's throat. On the end is a little tweezers that can grab things. Uncle Bob inserts the tube easily enough, but the challenge is getting a grip on the hook. The room is completely dark except for the image of Ferret's stomach on the TV screen. Dr. Dan and Fitz and a few other technicians watch, and no one makes a sound. Uncle Bob is more serious than usual, and I can see in the glow of the TV that he is starting to sweat.

"I can't get a good grip on this thing," he says after four or five failed attempts to grasp the toy.

He pulls the tube out a little and reinserts it into Ferret's belly. On the screen I can see the hook very clearly now.

"There," Uncle Bob says. "That's a better view." When he finally gets ahold of the hook, he slowly pulls it up. The whole thing reminds me of that game "Operation," where it buzzes if you touch the sides while trying to take out an organ. I keep expecting to hear a buzz as I see the hook moving up the esophagus and finally out of the mouth.

"We did it," Uncle Bob says with a big smile now. "And I think this ferret finally has a name—Hook." He holds up the toy. Dr. Dan pats him on the back and switches on the light. The room breaks out in applause as we all move in closer to have a look at the tiny orange plastic hook. It looks like a charm you get from a quarter machine at the grocery store.

"I can't believe how small it is," I comment.

"Yeah," Fitz says. "Hard to believe that something so small can cause such a big problem."

I stay with Ferret, or Hook, until he is brought back to the Intensive Care Unit and placed on a soft pad in one of the glass cages. He looks so small compared to some of the other animals on the unit, especially Samson, the Great Dane, just a few cages below. Samson is up and eating, and I ask Ray, the vet tech on duty, if it's okay to open his cage.

"Of course," he says, coming over to help me. "You

might want to say good-bye. Samson will be going home tomorrow." Ray reaches down and pats him on the head. "We were worried about this big fella."

I sit down on the floor just outside the cage and reach in to rub Samson's belly. He rolls over for more. He's so big his feet bang the top of the cage, and his tail wags so furiously it sounds like a thunderstorm.

"Who's making all that racket?" Uncle Bob calls from the door to the unit. He is holding his briefcase and jacket. "You ready to go home?"

"Sure," I say. "I just have one more good-bye."

I head back to the yellow room, the kennels. Bingo's sleeping in his cage. I don't want to disturb him, so I just look at him for a few minutes. Seeing him asleep makes me feel even more sorry for him.

"Don't worry," I whisper. "I'll find you a home."

Then I turn to Happy, who's still sitting on the metal twig.

"Won't we, Happy?" I say. "We'll find Bingo a home."

"Janelle, get out of town," she says as I'm just about out the door.

Chapter 4

My First Emergency

THE NEXT DAY IS EVEN busier than the first. Uncle Bob and I don't even make it to rounds because as soon as we pull into the parking lot, we notice two police cars and the Animal Control van.

"Looks like a hit-by," Uncle Bob says, hopping out of the car as fast as he can.

"What's a hit-by?"

"A dog or cat hit by a car," he says as we dash into the hospital.

In Treatment, the royal-blue room, there's hardly room for me. Almost every doctor and tech in the hospital is working around the treatment table, which is covered with blood.

I'm scared. I was hoping to see a real emergency, but

this one is *too* real. I've never seen Uncle Bob look serious.

It turns out that it isn't a hit-by.

"It's a bullet," Dr. Knor tells Uncle Bob.

"A bullet?" Uncle Bob asks. "How did that happen?"

"All we know is that a cop shot him," Dr. Fitz says.

"We don't even know the dog's name," Carole says. "Are there tags?"

"Here are some," Janelle says, and cuts off the dog's collar.

Meanwhile Dr. Petersen is working furiously to stop the bleeding and locate the bullet. "I'm afraid he may have severed an artery," he tells Uncle Bob. Then he turns to Janelle. "Hand me the towels, please. I can't see."

The dog is whimpering a bit, obviously uncomfortable.

"He's not too shocky," Uncle Bob says. He pats the dog's head and says, "It's all right, boy. It's all right."

I wonder what "shocky" means, but I know now is not a good time to ask. In fact, I feel like I shouldn't be here at all. Uncle Bob is shaking his head and running his hands through his hair. I know this means he's thinking, because that's exactly what my dad does when he thinks hard.

"Should we tranquilize him a bit to get some films?" Uncle Bob asks Dr. Petersen.

"First I think we need to turn him over and elevate the leg a little to slow down the bleeding."

"Okay," Uncle Bob says. "Let's get some hands. Janelle and Holly, take the front end, please. On the count of three, let's flip him."

I have to force myself to watch. Up until now I haven't had much of a view of the dog, because of all the people standing around him. Now that the four of them are behind him, I can see he's a big dog. Some sort of shepherd mix, I think, with a sweet white stripe running down the length of his snout. He cries and struggles as the four of them flip him over. Blood spurts from somewhere, and my heart races. I feel helpless. My first emergency seems like one too many already.

"Can someone clip his leg, please?" Dr. Petersen calls out. "I can't see anything with all this fur."

"Sure," Janelle says, and within thirty seconds his right hind leg is completely bare.

It's amazing to see how everyone's working together. Carole found a phone number on one of the tags.

"This is always the worst part," she says. "There's no easy way to tell someone their dog has been hurt."

I listen as she tells the owner—a Chris Hambidge—that there's been a little trouble. "We are stabilizing him now, but if there's any way you or a family member could come down, that would be great." After she hangs up she looks relieved. "He seemed nice. I think this one has a good owner."

"Did you get the dog's name?" Uncle Bob asks.

"His name is Roscoe."

"Roscoe, buddy," Dr. Petersen says. "It's okay, Roscoe."

Roscoe perks up a little at the mention of his name. The way they have him positioned now, his head is sticking out while they work on his leg. He looks at me with the saddest eyes I've ever seen. I decide that maybe I can help and walk over to pat his head. "Hi, Roscoe," I say.

Dr. Petersen tells Uncle Bob that the police officer who shot Roscoe is still out front. "I'm sure he'd love to get an update, and it would be great to get the whole story from him."

Uncle Bob goes out to talk to the policeman. I follow because I don't want to be in here petting a shot dog without my uncle nearby. It's not like it matters—in the midst of all this chaos I don't think anyone even knows I'm here. That's one thing I hate about being a kid—people don't notice you half the time.

The policeman sits in one of the orange waiting-room chairs. He's a small man with a big mustache. So big it seems it might tip his face right over if he's not careful. One hand twists his mustache while one foot taps the floor.

"Good morning, Officer, I'm Bob Taylor. We're working on the dog right now, trying to get the bleeding under control."

"I didn't mean to hurt him, Dr. Taylor. I was protecting a small boy."

"I have no doubt that you were doing your job, Officer . . ."

"Sadwith."

"Yes, Officer Sadwith. I just want to get a little information that might help us treat the dog. Was it just one shot you fired?"

"Yes, of course, just one. I was only trying to scare him. You know, hit the ground around his feet . . . but I hit him."

Uncle Bob turns to Carole at Reception. "Carole, tell Steve one bullet. And to look for an exit wound."

Uncle Bob spends at least fifteen more minutes talking with the police officer. Apparently Roscoe escaped from his fenced-in yard and found his way into a neighbor's yard, where a small child was playing. The child's father called the police. When the police arrived, the dog wouldn't move away from the child. It stood off to the side of him, growling. The father panicked and ran toward the child. Then the dog went for the dad. The police officer had no choice.

It's hard to believe that a dog like Roscoe would threaten anyone. I wander back to Treatment to see how he is doing and find that he is on his way to X-ray. Dr. Petersen found the exit wound and is eager to get an idea of how badly the leg is hurt. Ray, the X-ray technician, helps Dr. Petersen transfer Roscoe to a stretcher. I really like Ray. He doesn't say much, but when he does, it's usually funny. He doesn't want me in the room when he's taking the films. In fact, he doesn't even want me in the hallway. "You're too young and beautiful, pipsqueak," he says. Uncle Bob must have told him he didn't want me hanging around X-ray, because of the radiation.

I go back out front, where Uncle Bob is finishing up with the police officer. I hear him say, "Let me reiterate, Officer, this does not in any way appear to be a vicious animal."

That's what I thought! Roscoe let me pet him on the stretcher just a minute ago, and he gave Steve Petersen a kiss on the way into X-ray.

Officer Sadwith has to get back to work and fill out a

My First Emergency

complete report, but he promises to come back to check on Roscoe. Soon after he leaves, another man comes in. From the look in his eye Carole knows exactly who it is.

"Mr. Hambidge, I'm Carole Woodland. I called you earlier. Roscoe is stable now—he's getting some X-rays. Why don't you come on back to Exam Room Five, and I'll get Dr. Petersen to come out and have a few words with you."

"Can I see Roscoe?" he asks with panic in his voice.

"I'm sure Dr. Petersen will bring you back. Just let me tell him you're here. And keep in mind that Roscoe is in the best of care."

Carole's voice is so calm and reassuring that I can see Mr. Hambidge relax as he sits down in the exam room. Exam Room Five is the discussion room. It's the least clinical looking, with a few big comfortable chairs and a desk instead of a stainless-steel examination table.

"Can I get you something to drink while you wait, Mr. Hambidge?" Carole asks in her reassuring tone. I wonder how she does it, day after day, patient after patient. I really like Carole, and I like her work area, too. It's right up front so she can greet everyone who comes in, but it's hers and hers alone. The walls around her desk are filled with sayings on just about every subject. My two favorites are: "It's a dog-eat-dog world," and "Be yourself. Who else is better qualified?" Some of the staff affectionately call her "Carole Quote," because she always seems to have something philosophical to say. When I was little, Dad used to tell me that Mom had become one of God's angels. He swore that sometimes she spoke to him through other people. Maybe Carole's one of the people that carry the messages and lessons we all need to learn.

Uncle Bob and Dr. Petersen join Mr. Hambidge in Room Five. Since Janelle gave me the chore of sweeping the front area, and since the door is slightly ajar, I am able to get the gist of what's happening. Roscoe needs surgery to save his leg and Dr. Petersen wants to do it right away. It's a kind of surgery that Dr. Petersen and Uncle Bob specialize in. They'll put a pin into Roscoe's shattered bone to hold it together while the bone and muscles heal. Roscoe's owner wants to save the dog's leg. He's got another problem, though. Apparently the neighbor feels that Roscoe is now a threat to the neighborhood and thinks the dog should not come home, ever.

I don't know what Uncle Bob and Dr. Petersen say to Mr. Hambidge after that, because a dog howling in the waiting room makes it impossible to hear. I do catch Uncle Bob whispering to Dr. Petersen on their way back to surgery, "Our job is to stay focused on the animal." Then he turns to me and says, "Sorry, hon, looks like I'm going to be busy for a while."

My First Emergency   43

• • •

While Roscoe is in surgery, something strange happens. Carole finds a goose in the waiting room. It is sitting in a box and has a little note tied loosely around its neck. "Help," it reads. "I'm having trouble keeping up with the rest of the gang."

"Aren't we all," Carole jokes as she carries the goose in the box over to the reception desk.

"Where did you come from, Goose?" Dr. Knor asks as she walks out to meet her three-thirty appointment.

"Did you see who dropped it off, Megan?" Dr. Santen asks.

"No, I didn't." I'm embarrassed to tell everybody that I was too busy sweeping to notice when the goose was left.

"Apparently you really get into your work." Fitz says, now joining the crowd gathered around the goose.

I laugh and watch as Fitz picks up the goose. As soon as he lifts it out of the box, I can see that one leg is drooping down in a rather pathetic way.

"Well, it's pretty obvious," Fitz says. "This goose is"—he pauses—"cooked."

Dr. Santen, Holly, Carole, and a room full of waiting clients burst out laughing. But I'm worried about the goose. Uncle Bob doesn't treat birds. Aside from Happy, who squawks all day in the kennels, I haven't seen a single bird in here. I've learned that bird patients get referred to Dr. Shelby in Littleton. But there's no owner in this case—Goose has been abandoned.

"This looks like a case for Birdy," Dr. Fitz says.

"Who's Birdy?" I ask.

"She's a woman who takes care of all the birds in Denver," Holly tells me.

Dr. Fitz calls Birdy and asks her to come over. "Her real name is Katherine Hurlbutt," he says as we wait for her to arrive. "But for as long as I can remember, everybody's called her Birdy." Fitz says he's known Birdy since he was my age. "She's a sort of legend in Denver. A bird legend."

When I meet her, I'm a little surprised. She's an older woman—somewhere near eighty, I think. She drives around in what looks like a taxicab with pictures of birds all over the doors and hood. Dr. Fitzgerald says she's been around birds her whole life and knows them better than anyone in town. I hope she can help this goose.

When she talks, she even sounds a little like a bird. "What have we got here?"

"Birdy, this goose was left right here with a note saying he was having trouble keeping up with the rest of the gang," Dr. Fitz explains.

"Is that right?" Birdy chirps as she picks up the goose. "No wonder she's having trouble."

"Her leg's broken," Dr. Fitz says. "I'll put a splint on it."

"That'll be great. Hopefully she won't fuss with it too much."

Birdy tells me that birds are very sensitive creatures. The slightest disruption in their routine can kill them. "They often refuse to eat when they are injured. They are selfless creatures and don't want to bring the rest of the family down. But I can tell this one and I are going to get along fine. I'll get her to eat," she says as she places the goose back in the box.

I ask Birdy how she came to like birds so much.

"I'm not exactly sure, but maybe it's because my own wings are clipped. The only way for me to fly is through them."

I like Birdy and feel a little sad when I see her white taxi pull out. The license plate reads CBIRDS. She reminds me a little of my grandmother Mimi. She lived just a few blocks from me in Santa Rosa until she died last August. Mimi loved animals, too. She used to feed all the neighborhood cats.

Thinking of Mimi's strays reminds me of another stray—Bingo.

Bingo gets up and comes to the cage door as soon as he sees me. He knows I'll take him out. "Bingo," I say. "How's my Bingo?"

"I'm good, Megan," I hear from behind the wall of cages.

It's Matt, the head of Maintenance at Alameda East. He's responsible for making sure the place stays clean and well lit. Uncle Bob says he has one of the most important jobs.

"Very funny, Matt."

"So you found a friend, huh?" He gestures toward Bingo.

"A great one," I say. "I just wish we knew where he came from."

"You and the rest of us."

Roscoe's surgery takes a long time, and when it's over Uncle Bob spends more time consulting with Dr. Petersen. Then he calls Mr. Hambidge and Officer Sadwith with updates on Roscoe's condition. By the time he's ready to call it quits, it's pretty late, and we're both beat.

On the drive home I ask Uncle Bob about Birdy. "She doesn't live very far from the hospital," he tells me. "And her house is incredible—birds everywhere. Maybe you could visit her while you're here."

"That'd be great."

Then we talk about Roscoe. "How do you do it?" I say. "I was scared. I felt so bad watching him bleed."

"I was scared, too, Megan."

"Yeah, but at least you could do something to help the dog. All I could do was pet him, and that's not going to get him well."

"It's a start. You know, there are a lot of people who wouldn't be able to pet a dog that had been shot and was bleeding that badly."

As soon as we get home, I take a shower. The warm water feels so good on my tired body, and I start to feel better. Even a little hungry. It's already so late that Allison and Tommy are asleep. Dad knew that some days at the hospital would be long. "Don't push it, though," he'd said. "No more than one late night a week."

Aunt Barbara has dinner all ready for me.

"How's my young vet?" she says. "Bob says it was a hard day."

I tell her about Roscoe and how we're all worried that he might be put to sleep. "I think he thought that something was wrong."

"It's hard to understand sometimes when animals act aggressively," Aunt Barbara says sympathetically.

"That's for sure." But there must be a good explanation in this case. I know in my heart that Roscoe's not a bad dog.

Later, just when I'm about to fall asleep, I sit bolt upright in bed. I've already been in Denver two whole days and I haven't written to Sarah yet! She's going to kill me. I have so much to tell her, about Roscoe, Bingo, Ferret, the doctors. . . . Oh well, I'm too tired to do it now. I'll do it tomorrow, Sarah, I promise.

Chapter 5

Pat the Hyena

Dear Sarah:

See? I've gotten better about writing to you. It's easier to do it first thing in the morning, when I'm not so tired.

Today I'm not going to Alameda East. Instead I'm going down to the zoo with Uncle Bob. He's going to operate on a hyena. It's the same surgery Uncle Bob and Dr. Petersen performed on Roscoe, but today I don't even want to think about Roscoe. It's all gotten so complicated. The hospital is not allowed to release Roscoe until a judge signs a paper saying it's okay, and the judge can't sign the paper because the neighbor wants Roscoe to be put to sleep. Roscoe's owner, Chris Hambidge, is fighting the whole thing with a countersuit. He thinks Roscoe was trying to protect the kid from an intruder who'd been in the neighborhood.

• • •

Uncle Bob and I talk about Roscoe's case on the way to the zoo. Everyone at the hospital wants the dog back with its owner. "It's hard, though, because I can certainly see the neighbor's point of view, too," Uncle Bob says. "Animals both domestic and wild will attack when threatened. It's instinct. Animal nature."

Instinct. Animal nature. I've been thinking a lot about these words, wondering if that's all there is to animals. Yesterday, during my third round of sweeping, I watched a cat play in the front lobby. He hid behind a chair, eyeing a ball of yarn his owner dangled in front of him. With teasing paws the cat reached out and tried to grab the ball while the owner pulled the string and the ball leaped up. This went on for a while, until the owner got into a conversation with a woman sitting next to her. She stopped pulling the yarn and the ball lay still. With a look of fierce determination the cat pounced on the defenseless ball as if to kill it. I wondered for a minute then if animals were even nice at all. Maybe all the behavior we think of as cute and loving is really just instinct. Then I thought of Roscoe licking Dr. Petersen on the way to X-ray, and of Bingo, who had fast become my best friend out here in Denver. There is more to these animals than instinct. There is an innocence, a purity.

I ask Uncle Bob if I'll be able to pet the hyena.

"Only when he's unconscious, which should be most of the time."

"You mean I might never see him awake?"

Uncle Bob tells me that the people at the zoo have to tranquilize an animal even to get it out of its cage. "We don't want to put too much stress on the animal, and of course we don't want you to get hurt."

That makes sense to me. I can't complain—how many other kids have gotten this close to a hyena?

The entrance we use is in the back, a good quarter mile from the public entrance. We ring a doorbell shaped like an elephant's snout and we're buzzed in with no questioning. Once inside, I see a golf cart waiting for us. The driver doesn't look much older than me.

"Hi, Dr. Taylor," the boy says.

"Hi, Peter."

"Dr. Kenney is ready and waiting. Pat's ready, too."

I don't know who Dr. Kenney or Pat is. Right now I'm focused on our driver. He seems too young to be driving.

"Megan, this is Dr. Kenney's son, Peter. He works here every summer. Isn't that right?"

"Yes, sir."

"Wow, that's cool," I say. Almost as cool as what I'm doing this summer, I think.

When we get to the zoo's clinic, I find out that Pat is the hyena and Dr. Kenney is the head doctor at the zoo. He'll be working with Uncle Bob during the surgery.

"Would you like to pet Pat, Megan?" Dr. Kenney asks.

"Sure. Is Pat a boy or a girl?"

"Funny you should ask," Dr. Kenney says. He explains that a hyena's sex organs are hidden, so unless the animal is opened surgically, it's almost impossible to tell if it is a male or a female. "That's why we call all our hyenas Pat."

"Is that true?" I ask. "That's funny."

Pat is in an area called Induction, which from what I gather is where they give it anesthesia, or a sleeping drug. To me Pat looks like a girl. With her eyes closed I can see long lashes that make her look almost pretty. Dr. Kenney says now would be the best time to pet Pat, because once she goes into the operating room, everyone who touches her has to be sterile—clean and germ-free. All I can think of while I'm petting Pat is how I wish I could hear her laugh.

I ask Dr. Kenney what happened to her. He says the reason she needs this operation is that Peter ran her over with the cart not too long ago.

"Did not!" Peter protests.

"Well, you certainly could have, the way you drive that thing," Dr. Kenney teases him. "Actually, Pat got into a fight with one of the other Pats. She was injured trying to get away from her attacker, who has since been put into isolation."

So I was right—this Pat is a girl.

The operation takes a little over two hours. Perched on a high stool, I watch through a window. It's easy to forget that Uncle Bob is operating on a wild animal from Africa.

"So, what do you think?" Peter asks, interrupting my thoughts.

"It's neat," I say.

"It's going to take them a while to stitch her up. If you want, I can take you for a ride around the zoo." He pauses. "I can show you the rest of the Pats."

"That'd be great. But are you sure it's safe for me to drive with you?"

"Of course it is," Peter says with a laugh. "My dad was just kidding. Besides, I've already got my learner's permit."

Peter tells me he is sixteen plus five months and seventeen days. "I'm counting," he says. "Only one hundred and ninety-six days until I get my license."

The first area we visit is the hyenas' habitat. I see three hyenas lying on a brown patch of grass. They seem hot and listless.

"Are the Pats okay?"

"They're fine. Most of the animals are more active at night, after the zoo closes. And Dad was just kidding about the names, too. They're not all called Pat, though we do try and give them names that could be used for both male and female."

The three hyenas in front of me are Chris, Fran, and Joe.

Peter takes me to the elephants next, then we go to see the lions and the seals. The seals are my favorite, maybe because they are the first bunch that seem awake. It's feeding time. A big crowd has gathered around to watch, but we have no trouble seeing. Peter has parked the cart around the back side of the aquarium. We're actually sitting right behind the girl who is feeding the seals.

The last animal Peter takes me to see is his favorite, a giraffe named Hannah.

"Hannah's not just any giraffe," he says.

And it's true. Hannah is the most unusual giraffe I have ever seen. Instead of yellow with brown spots, she is all white.

"Is she sick?" I ask him.

"No, she just doesn't have much pigment in her skin. She's an albino giraffe."

"I bet she needs to stay out of the sun."

"That's true. It's funny, but she knows this instinctively. While the other giraffes stay out all day, she usually stays inside."

On the ride back to the operating room, Peter tells me about some of the medical emergencies he's seen while working at the zoo.

"The scariest was when a mountain goat somehow escaped from the habitat, walked out of the gate, and was hit by a car."

"What did you do?"

"Well, as luck would have it, the people that hit her brought her to Alameda East."

"The people just put her in the car?" I ask, amazed. "A mountain goat?"

"Yup."

"I think I might have called for help first," I tell Peter.

"Me, too."

When Peter and I get back to the operating area, I see that Pat has been moved to a cage. She's just waking up. She moves groggily around the steel cell, staggering as if she is drunk. Every once in a while she bangs her head on the metal wall.

"Oh, poor thing."

"She'll be fine, Megan," Uncle Bob says, putting his arm around me. "Come on, let's go home."

We leave the same way we arrived, through the secret entrance.

In the car I lean over and give Uncle Bob a hug. "Thanks," I say. "This has been the best day so far."

When he smiles, Uncle Bob looks just like my dad.

Chapter 6

Hanging Out with Holly

THE NEXT DAY AT ROUNDS, Fitz makes a big announcement. Roscoe is going home. Chris Hambidge, his owner, called late last night to say that an intruder *had* been in the neighborhood—the police had caught him. The neighbor dropped the charges against Roscoe. He just asked that Roscoe be put on a long leash when Chris is away during the day.

"Thank God," Uncle Bob says, and the rest of the staff claps. I smile from ear to ear.

I spend the rest of the morning in the surgery prep room, helping Janelle and the interns sterilize the surgical equipment. Janelle supervises the interns, about twenty students from the local vet-tech school. Each one is finishing up a two-year associate degree program. This is their first experience out in the field. After they finish the internship they'll be ready to work as certified veterinary technicians. I can relate to the interns. They're also pretty new around here, and they want to be helpful. They talk to me about the differences between learning in the class and learning in the field. "The first time I had to draw blood," Shelly says, "I almost fainted."

"You should have seen me during my first surgery," Kim says. "I *did* faint."

I like listening to their stories as we fold what look like giant cloth dinner napkins over stainless-steel surgical ware. First we put in two scalpel blade handles, then a tong, two probes, and a mirror. We fold the napkin over, tuck the ends in, then roll it and place it in a pile. The pile then goes into the oven. It's not the kind of oven you make cookies in. It's a sterilization oven, and it's very important to the hospital's practice. The vets have to make sure that everything is sterile, because when an animal comes in for surgery, it is at its most vulnerable. A dirty instrument could give it a disease.

"In surgery, an animal isn't even breathing on his own. We're doing that for him," Janelle tells me. "Then we open him up, usually cutting through bone and muscle, so he's real susceptible to infection."

After all the talk about fainting, I start to feel a little queasy at this description. I try to change the subject.

"What's that?" I ask, pointing to a machine that looks like the hose at the dentist's office.

"Oh, that's a suction machine. We use that during surgery to clear away blood and tissue that might obstruct the surgeon's work."

"Ugh," I say, again feeling her words in my stomach.

Janelle tells me that Uncle Bob and Dr. Petersen, the board-certified surgeons, use the suction machine the most. They do bone and tissue repair, as well as microsurgery.

"What does Dr. Santen do?" I ask.

"He is the inside doctor. You can think of him as Alameda's detective—he's the one who is going to diagnose what's going on inside your dog. If a dog has a runny nose, he can tell whether it's a cold or a possible tumor. He solves mysteries, while Dr. Knor and Dr. Fitzgerald are our general practitioners. They are detectives, too, but they also do regular checkups as well as spays and neuters."

"I know all about spays and neuters from working at the Humane Society," I tell her. "Every animal there had to be fixed; otherwise, they couldn't be adopted."

"Yeah, we have too many dogs and cats without homes as it is," she says.

"Like Bingo?"

"Exactly, like Bingo," Janelle says.

Along with supervising the vet techs and interns, Janelle's in charge of all the strays that come in.

"We had twenty-four last month," she tells me.

"Twenty-four? Where did they end up?"

"Ten went back to their original owners. Six we adopted out, and the rest went to the shelter."

"Will Bingo go to the shelter?" I ask.

"If we don't find his owner and if no one here can adopt him."

I feel sick hearing this. Even though I've only been here a week, I've fallen in love with Bingo. I think he's kind of my Dixie fill-in.

"When?" I ask.

"Well, let's see. He's been here almost two weeks and our limit is thirty days."

"Thirty days? That would mean Bingo is only here for another two weeks."

I'm going to be an intern almost another five weeks, and the thought of being here without my pal makes me sad.

Janelle interrupts my thoughts. "We can probably stretch it to forty-five days. Come on, Megan. Speaking of Bingo, let's go give him a walk."

We go back to the yellow room, where the kennels are. Since it's close to walk time, all the dogs are barking. Only the blood donors are quiet. I guess they've been here long enough to know the routine and to trust that their needs will be met at some point.

Bingo squeals with delight when he sees me. When Janelle opens the cage, he leaps past her into my arms. We laugh.

"I can see who he favors," Janelle says.

I like hanging out with Janelle. She's easy to talk to, and she cares so much for all the animals.

"Janelle," I ask her, "what do you think of the blood donors? I think it's kind of a sad life."

"They're not unhappy, Megan . . . and this one," she says, pointing to an orange and white tabby cat, "this one is going home soon. Terry—one of the vet techs—is taking her."

"That's great," I say, feeling a whole lot better.

After our walk Janelle tells me, "I'm going to hand you off to Dr. Knor now. By today I think you're familiar enough to be assigned a certain area or doctor, like the regular interns. In addition to having some other regular duties, like waiting-room cleanup and stuff like that."

"That's great, Janelle. Just great."

• • •

I meet up with Dr. Knor in Treatment.

"You're just in time," she says. "I'm about to see a puppy who got into a leftover Easter basket—a chocolate one. She ate the whole thing."

I follow Dr. Knor up to the front, where a woman named Agnes sits with an adorable golden-retriever puppy. Agnes looks like she could have gotten into the chocolate herself. She has a certain look of mischief in her eye, just like her dog, Razzle, who sits beside her, panting and wagging her tail.

"How long ago did Razzle eat the chocolate?" Dr. Knor asks.

"Oh," Agnes tells her, "it couldn't have been more than a half hour ago."

"Good," says Dr. Knor. "Then it's no problem at all."

Dr. Knor explains to Agnes that we're going to take Razzle in the back and give her a drug called apomorphine. "This will make her vomit."

"What a shame," Agnes says. "It was a lovely basket."

Dr. Knor lets me take Razzle's leash and lead her back to Treatment. She bounces after me without the least look of apprehension in her eyes.

In Treatment, Dr. Knor asks Terry to prep the apomorphine. Terry takes Razzle over to the scale because it's very important to weigh an animal before any medication is given out. It's the only way to know how much to give.

"Apomorphine is kind of like Ipecac syrup," Dr. Knor says to me. "Have you heard of Ipecac?"

"Oh, yes. Dad always has it in the house in case I eat something bad."

"Well, apomorphine works the same way. It induces vomiting. So, a few minutes after we give Razzle a shot, he'll throw up the Easter basket and anything else he's had in the past few hours. This way we'll keep him from having any ill effects from the chocolate."

Dr. Knor explains that chocolate contains an ingredient called theobromide, which can cause a reaction in animals that is sometimes fatal.

"Dogs should just never have chocolate. It can kill them," Holly says.

"Any kind of chocolate?" I ask, remembering when Dixie got into the mini-pack of M&M's I had stuffed away in my knapsack last fall.

"It's usually baking chocolate that does it because that has more theobromides in it, but we don't take chances with any chocolate."

I'm glad Dixie didn't get enough to hurt her.

Terry puts Razzle on the table and hands Dr. Knor a syringe. "All set, Dr. Knor."

"Well, Megan," the doctor says with a smile, "what goes down must come up."

I groan at Dr. Knor's joke and watch her put the needle into Razzle's front paw. She's obviously found a vein right away because I can see a little blood drop into the hub of the needle before she pushes the plunger into the syringe.

"There we go . . . should take effect in a minute or two."

Almost before she finishes her sentence, I see a change in Razzle. She no longer looks so happy to be here. A strange glossiness comes over her eyes. Then she sits up and her body starts to heave. Terry runs over to grab a barrel and puts it in front of Razzle's snout. Razzle is weaving a bit and I wonder if she'll even make her target. Then, with a thrust that seems like it will throw her off the table, she opens her mouth and vomits.

"Ugh," I cry, holding my stomach.

For a minute I'm sure I will throw up, too. I tend to throw up when I see other people throw up. Or gag at least. I wonder if this problem will keep me from getting through vet school. I look up and see that Holly—Dr. Knor—is not at all bothered. She might as well be eating a sandwich. Terry, same thing. Perfectly calm. They see me staring and begin to laugh.

"Don't worry, we all felt sick the first time," Terry says.

"Believe it or not, you'll get used to it." Dr. Knor adds. "Do you want to see what's in here?" she asks, pointing to the barrel.

"No way," I say.

"Oh, come on," she says. "She ate the ribbon and everything."

I look over at Razzle, who now appears as if nothing happened. Her tail is wagging.

"Hey, Razzle," I say. "Good job."

"I don't have any appointments after three," Holly tells me. "What do you say we visit Children's Hospital with Kingsley? Then I can drop you off at your uncle's house."

"I'd love to!"

Children's Hospital is only about a ten-minute drive away. I'm excited to be with Holly, but a little nervous about seeing sick kids. We drive in her purple Toyota pickup. Holly sings to songs on the oldies radio station as Kingsley hops back and forth between the backseat and the front seat, giving kisses to both of us.

"Kingsley's all excited," she tells me. "He knows where we're going."

That reminds me of the way Dixie always knows when we're going to the vet's office. As soon as we get off the turnpike and head up the main street in Santa Rosa, she starts to whimper. First it's only small whines, but by the time we pull into the parking lot, she is howling. I bet Kingsley and Kane, Holly's dogs, never whimper on the way to the vet's. Good thing, too—they'd be whimpering all the time, because they *live* with their vet.

Children's Hospital is bigger than I expected. It makes me sad that there are so many sick kids. I've never known any really sick kids, except for Teddy White, who was born with a hole in his heart. Lots of times he looked blue because he wasn't getting enough oxygen. He had an operation, though, and his family moved away shortly after that. I hear he's doing fine now, so I'm hoping there are kids like that in here—kids who are doing fine.

I don't like hospitals very much, but this one is different. There's a playground with swings right inside the front lobby, and Kingsley's not the only dog walking around. There's a poodle waiting for the elevator, and a small terrier mix walking into the store. Dogs really cheer up a place. I've often thought the grocery store would be a better place if you could bring your dog. Dad says it would be bedlam. All the food would be yanked off the shelves. I guess that's true, but still, it would be a whole lot more fun. And that's what being at Children's Hospital feels like to me, like being at the grocery store with your dog. I half expect someone in a uniform to come up behind us and scream, "Get that animal out of here!" Instead he is greeted by name. "Hi, Kingsley," the guard at the front desk says. "Good to see you today." Then he turns to Holly. "What floor would you like to hit today, Holly?"

"Orthopedics, if that's okay."

Holly tells me that Orthopedics is the most fun. There are usually kids who are feeling pretty good but have to stay still because they just got a fracture repaired. "So having the dog on the bed with them is a pretty big thrill."

Holly tells me a little bit about what Kingsley had to do in order to get this job. "It's pretty rigorous training," she says, and she describes what sounds like doggy boot camp. "First they put Kingsley in a narrow hallway and chased after him banging pots and pans."

"That sounds awful," I say, but she explains that the dogs that come here have to be unflappable.

"No animal instinct allowed at this place," she says. "Only love."

I wonder what makes some animals unflappable and others aggressive. I think Dixie could probably get through the training, but Roscoe? Forget it.

First we visit a little girl who's had her jaw repaired. She broke it in a car accident. She can't talk yet, but she pats the bed and Kingsley jumps up. He snuggles right next to her, and Holly pulls out a camera and tells them both to smile. It's a Polaroid camera, so the picture comes out right away. When the little girl sees it, her eyes light up, and she makes a small sound that must be a laugh. I look over her shoulder and see that Kingsley is actually smiling in the picture. His upper lip is curled up, and he looks like he's really posing.

The next boy we see had his leg reset. He broke it in four places after falling down a shaft at a local community center. I can tell he is uncomfortable. He is a little cranky when we first get there. Since Holly's a vet she knows a lot of medical terminology, and she talks to him about his symptoms.

He isn't listening. He's looking down and picking at his blanket.

"This is Kingsley, and I'm Holly, and this is Megan," Holly says in her cheeriest voice.

"Hi, Kingsley," the boy says, perking up a bit. He asks if Kingsley can come up and say hi.

"Just pat the bed," Holly says.

He does, and Kingsley jumps right up. He circles around a few times before curling up next to the boy's cast.

"Ouch," the boy says.

"Oh, no, did he hurt you?" Holly asks. "Kingsley, get down, boy."

The boy looks down again. He seems so sad.

"I broke my leg when I was seven," I tell him. "It was only in two places, but the bone went out of my skin. Would you like to see my scar?"

He lifts his head and smiles for the first time. "Sure, I'd like to see it. How long did it take to heal?"

"I don't remember exactly, but it wasn't too bad, I promise."

"The whole thing's just been a little scary," he says, now looking at Holly.

"Well, of course," she says. "I'd be scared, too."

Just then a lady walks in carrying an armful of snacks.

"Hi, Mom, this is Kingsley," he says, pointing at me. Then he points to the dog. "And this is Holly." Finally he points to Holly. "And this is Megan—she's had her leg broken in two places, and the bone went out of her skin."

Holly and I laugh. "And who are you?" Holly asks, looking at the boy's mother.

"I'm Ryan," his mother says. "And the boy over there in the bed is his mom."

Now we are all laughing.

When we leave Ryan, Holly bends down and gives me a hug. "You were great in there," she says. "I think you and Dixie ought to do this when you get back home. You're a natural with people."

I feel so happy when she says this to me. It's a great feeling to make a difference in someone's day. Holly tells me this is her favorite thing to do at lunch. "It's more filling than food."

By the time we leave the hospital, we've seen eleven children and taken fourteen Polaroids. I take one of Holly and Kingsley, and she takes one of Kingsley and me. "Let's get him to take one of us," I suggest, and we laugh.

"I have a better idea," she says, and on the way out she asks the guard if he can snap one of the three of us.

I hold the picture on the way home. Holly has already said that she wants me to keep it. I'm happy to have a memory of walking around the grocery store with the dog that smiles.

That night when I call Dad, he tells me that after sniffing around my bedroom for a week, Dixie finally settled down at the foot of his bed.

"Can you believe she slept with me, Meg?" he says.

"I don't believe it. . . . I guess I've been replaced," I kid.

"Never," Dad says.

I tell Dad about my day at Children's Hospital. He's

heard of these programs before. "They even have them in nursing homes and prisons," he says.

"Can we do it?" I ask. "Me and Dixie?"

"Only if I can come, too."

"Of course." I laugh. "Maybe sometime we can even get Holly to come. If she's in the neighborhood. She's really nice, Dad."

"Are you playing matchmaker again?"

"Well, maybe a little. Wait till you see her picture!"

"I can't wait to see *you*!" he says, changing the subject. "It seems like the days are going too slowly."

"Not for me, Dad. I've never been so busy." Then I quickly add, "But I miss you, too. Honest!"

Chapter 7

A Visit to the Bird House

THIS MORNING I'M THE "FLOATER." Each day Janelle assigns a different intern to be the floater, a position that doesn't involve any actual floating. The floater is an intern who is supposed to be on hand in case another intern gets sick or one of the doctors needs some extra hands. A lot of the interns complain about being the floater because it means that they have to clean out the kennels with Matt while they're waiting for other work. But I don't mind at all. With all my experience at the Humane Society, cleaning out cages is one task I know I can handle. Also, it means I get to be around Bingo all day.

My plan is to see if Bingo knows how to sit and stay. If he does know, Matt says it's okay for me to use him as sort of an assistant today. He can visit all the dogs with

A Visit to the Bird House

me, and when I clean out their cages, Bingo can hang out on the patio with them.

"Just be careful around that bird," Matt warns me. "You know how particular she is about our furry friends."

At this Happy squawks. "Yeah, you know who we are talking about," Matt says to her.

"Janelle, get out of town," Happy replies.

I laugh as I unlock Bingo's cage. "Come on, boy," I say. "I've got a test for you."

Bingo happily follows me out to the patio. I grab a few biscuits from the tin in the corner and begin my exam. "Sit." Bingo sits. "Come." Bingo comes. "Sit." Bingo sits. "Stay." Bingo stays. Even when I walk around the patio, he stays. "Bingo, stay," I say again, and then I let loose and dance around like a lunatic. Bingo still stays. "Wow, Bingo. Somebody trained you well. Good boy." I give him a big hug. "You want to be my assistant today?" He barks.

Bingo and I spend the morning cleaning cages. Bingo makes friends easily, but he is particularly fond of Terry's cat. He keeps going up to the cage and licking at her through the bars. It's cute.

Bingo makes another friend—Happy. Even though Matt says, "No, Bingo, come back," Bingo puts his nose to Happy's cage. "Janelle, get out of town," Happy squawks. Bingo wags his tail. Happy hops down off the twig and comes closer until Bingo and Happy are eye to eye.

"They like each other," I say.

"Seems that way," Matt agrees.

After lunch I'm excused from floater duty. Janelle tells me to shadow Dr. Fitz.

"I've got an exotic," he says with little-boy enthusiasm.

The exotic is an iguana named Iggy who belongs to a man named Ike. Iggy and Ike make quite a pair. Ike's hair is almost as long as Janelle's, and both of his arms are covered with tattoos of snakes, scorpions, lizards, and newts.

"Great artwork," Fitz says about the jungle on Ike's arms. Ike strikes me as being a tough guy, but Fitz doesn't seem at all uncomfortable around him.

"Is this Iggy?" Fitz asks, pointing to an iguana tattoo on Ike's lower arm.

"No, that's my other iguana, Harry. Harry died last year. Iggy was Harry's replacement."

"Oh yeah, of course. This one's got that little dimple in his chin," Fitz says as he lifts Iggy out of his carrier.

ALAMEDA EAST VETERINARY HOSPITAL

ANIMAL EMERGENCY ROOM
24 HOUR SERVICE

9870

This is the place!

The Vets

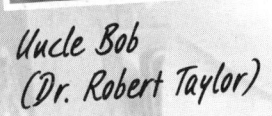

Uncle Bob
(Dr. Robert Taylor)

Dr. Kevin Fitzgerald

Dr. Doug Santen

Dr. Steve Petersen

Dr. Holly Knor

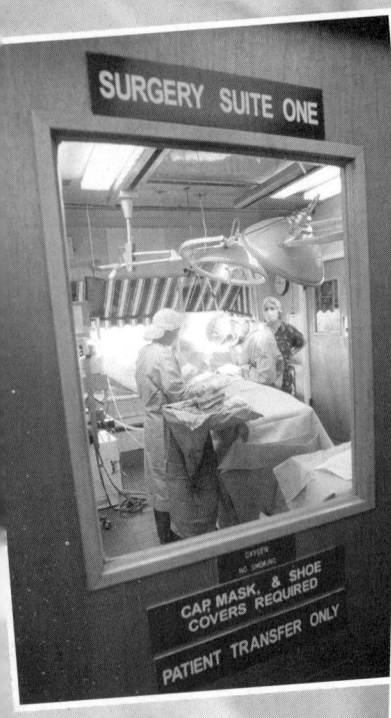

Hard at Work

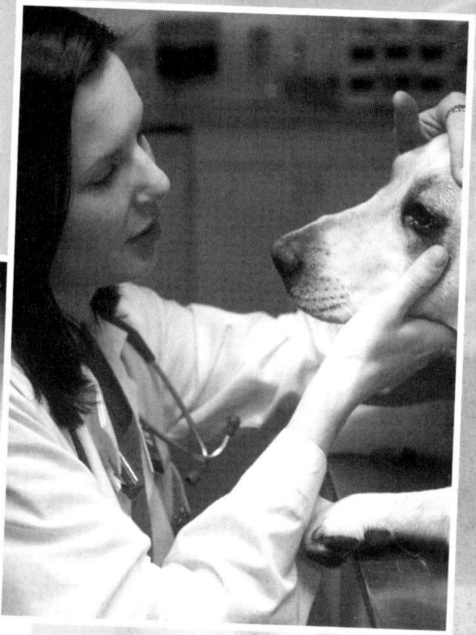

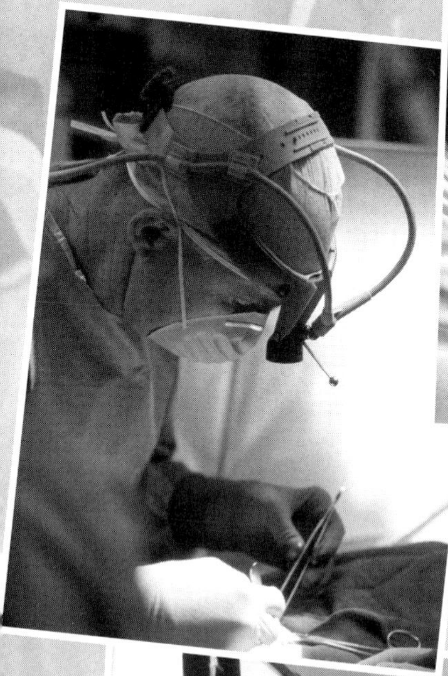

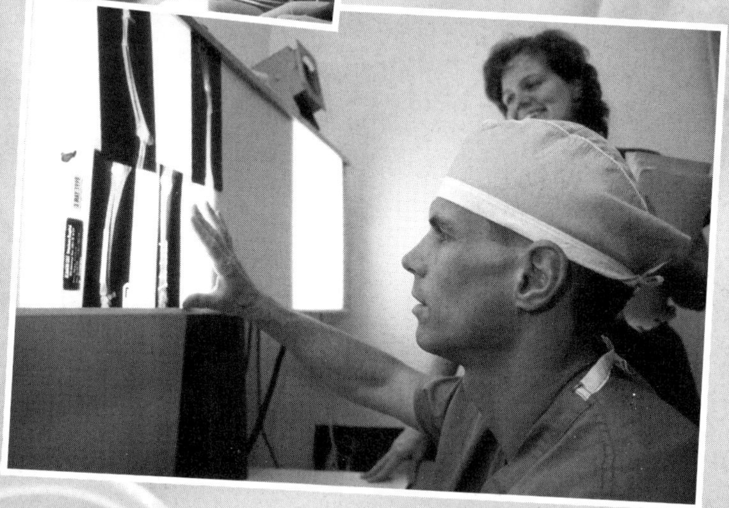

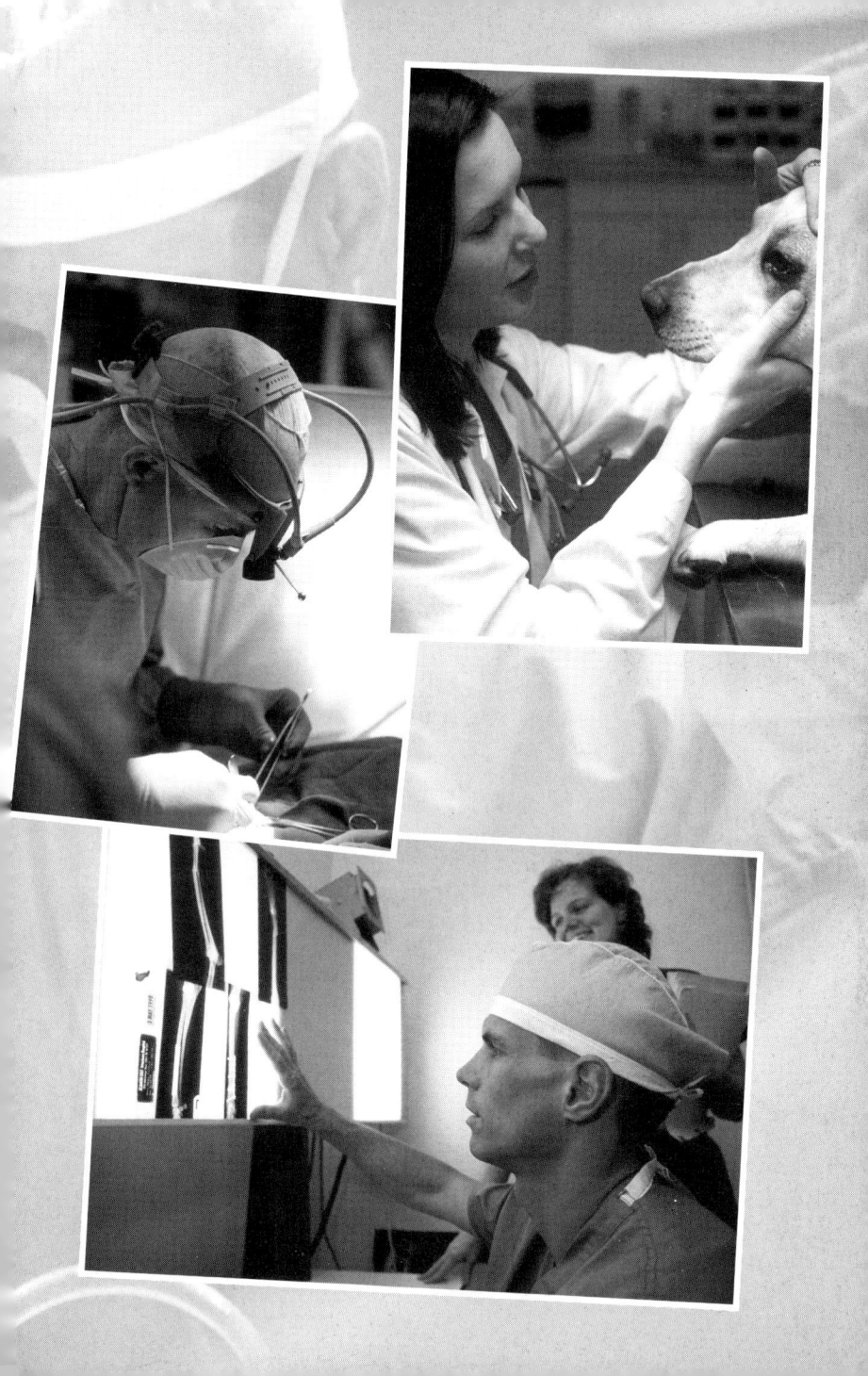

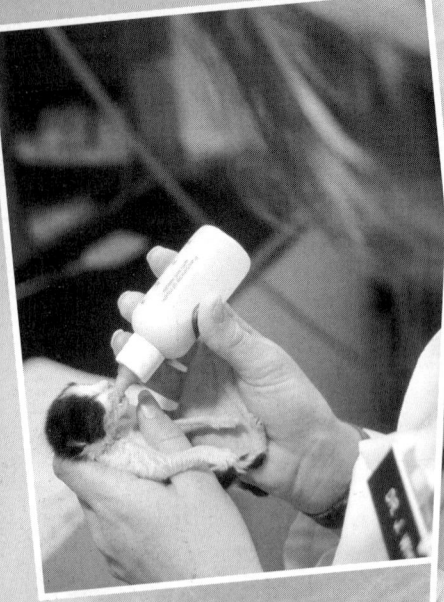

Tender Loving Care

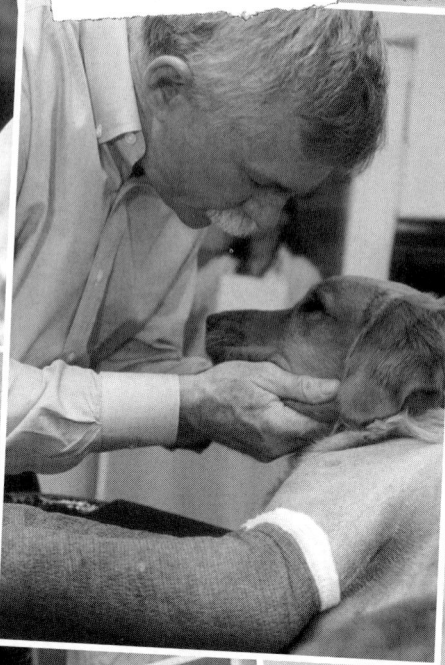

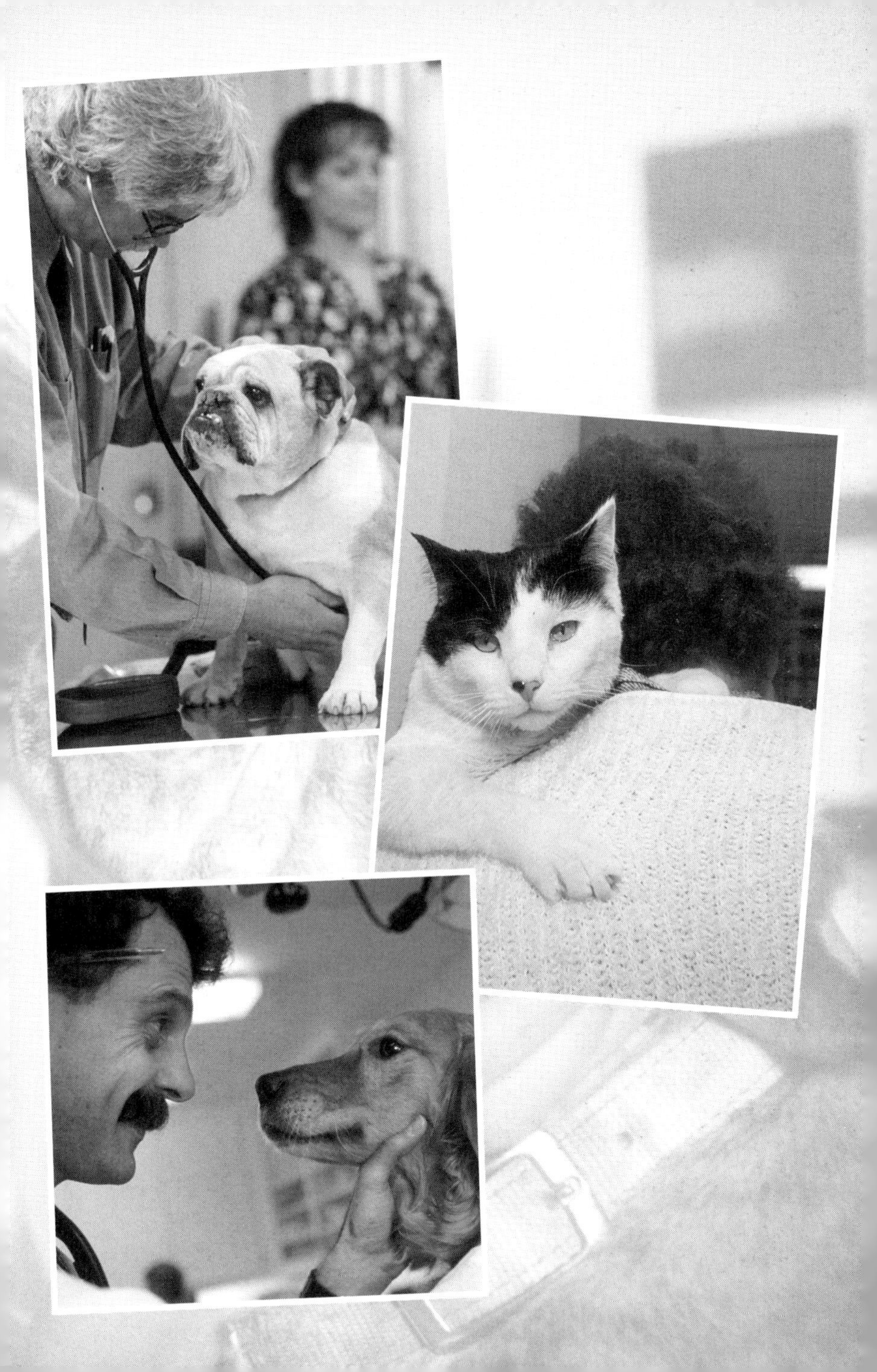

Best wishes to Megan from the staff at Alameda East. We'll miss you!

Ike smiles and suddenly looks a lot softer to me. He tells Fitz that Iggy has been lethargic. "Really not right since I bought him."

"Where did you get Iggy?" Fitz asks him.

"He's from Lizards' Den on Wadsworth."

"Sure, I know that place. That's a good place."

Fitz takes some time to examine Iggy. He checks his mouth and under his neck. Then he sort of props Iggy up on the exam table as he feels around his stomach.

"Did Rick sell you this guy?

"Yeah."

"Did he tell you this was a male?"

"I don't know."

"Because this guy is having some pretty big female trouble."

"Female trouble?" Ike looks confused. "What do you mean?"

"Well, Iggy's a female, and it's no wonder she's tired. If you were dropping as many eggs as she is, you'd be tired, too."

Fitz puts Iggy back in the carrier and covers it with a towel. He tells Ike that Iggy's eggs will need to be dissolved or removed. "See, what happens with these guys—I mean girls—is that if they don't lay their eggs, the eggs suck up all the calcium and other nutrients that

Iggy should be getting. So that's why you have a tired iguana. But the good news is we can fix it."

"How?" Ike asks.

"Well, the first thing we'll try is a few injections of a hormone that should stimulate Iggy to release the eggs. I can take her to Treatment and give her the shot, or you can wait a few minutes with her here and I can bring the shot back."

"You can take him—I mean her," Ike says.

"Great." Then Fitz turns to me. "Megan, why don't you get her."

"Okay." I reach into the carrier and put my hands around Iggy's belly. I might as well tell you now that I favor dogs, cats come in a close second, but reptiles don't even make it to my top ten. Holding this iguana by the belly is giving me a case of the willies. I think I may be squeezing too hard because I can feel her ribs, but if I don't, I think she might get away. I move one hand underneath her belly and I'm adjusting the other to support her tail when she jerks around and makes a noise that can only be described as nasty.

"Oh, no!" I scream, and I let go with the hand that's supporting her belly. Iggy begins to fall, but luckily I catch her by a back leg and she just hangs upside down for a second until Fitz grabs her.

A Visit to the Bird House

"Let me take that squirmy guy—I mean girl," Fitz says, and we walk out the door and down the hallway.

Fitz injects Iggy with a hormone called oxytocin. It stimulates muscle contractions, which will help Iggy get rid of these eggs.

"Basically we want her to 'give birth' to the eggs," he says. "But sometimes it doesn't work and we have to go in surgically. Kind of like a cesarean birth. Do you know what that is?"

"Sure," I say. "My best friend Sarah was born that way."

"Oxytocin takes a little while to work, so we'll let Ike take her home and see if she drops any of these eggs."

Fitz also gives Iggy an injection of calcium along with some saline and dextrose—salt and sugar water. With all these eggs inside her, Iggy is in danger of dehydrating.

After Iggy leaves, Fitz and I talk. I'm so embarrassed about dropping her that I can barely look at him.

"Megan, I've dropped them all," he says. "Besides, you had her by the leg, didn't you?"

I ask Fitz how come he's always so nice. "I was kind of scared of Iggy's owner at first," I admit.

"You get used to working with all kinds of people, Megan. The one thing all owners have in common is love for their pet. I try to win their trust and their pet's trust. The pets don't judge me, and I don't judge them. Then I take their owner's money, and their owners judge me. They think I'm a crook."

"The nicest crook," I say.

"Well, you'll be the nicest crook, too, someday."

On the way home that night Uncle Bob takes me by Birdy's to check on Goose. Birdy lives in a typical suburban neighborhood, but there isn't anything typical about what goes on at her house. As soon as I walk into her living room, I am greeted by a raven named Edgar.

"Never," he says.

"Won't you be good?" Birdy asks him.

"Never," he says again.

There isn't a stick of furniture in the living room, the dining room, or the second bedroom. Only large cages with birds inside. The only room that looks like a person uses it is Birdy's bedroom, and even that is pretty spare. It has only a twin bed and a desk with a phone and an answering machine.

"You want to see your goose, I bet," she says as she starts walking toward the back of the house. "Well, come outside."

We walk through a screened-in porch that is filled with

at least a hundred pigeons. She stops and points to one of the ceiling beams in the corner. "Look at that," she says. "Beautiful, isn't it?"

I look up and see a circle of twigs and sticks neatly entwined—a nest.

"See how the center is caved down a bit?" Birdy says. "It's a perfect bowl. A bowl for eggs."

Now I notice three little eggs cupped in the center of this perfect little nest. I never thought about it before, but a nest *is* pretty beautiful.

Out in the backyard we find the injured goose. He is cruising around in a "birdie" wheelchair.

"How did you do this?" Uncle Bob asks Birdy.

"It really is amazing," I add.

"Oh, it's nothing," Birdy says. "Just rearranged some toys is all."

It looks like Birdy used the wheels from a toy doll carriage, fastened material around the frame, and cut out little holes for the goose's legs.

We stay for almost an hour before Uncle Bob realizes that it's after seven o'clock. "We better get you home. Your aunt is going to kill me."

Birdy tells me to come by anytime. "Now that you know where I am, there's no excuse. Besides, I could use a hand."

When we get home, Allison and Aunt Barbara are watching a documentary on TV about a red panda. It's the story of a little cub named Pan Pan whose mother is struggling to keep him safe from predators.

"Did you know that pandas eat their babies?" Allison tells me.

"No, they don't."

"They do if they think someone else is going to hurt them."

"Sick," I say. "What are these animals thinking?"

I head upstairs, needing a few minutes free from animals. Up in my room I find an envelope on the bed. It's a letter from Dad. In it is a picture of Dixie lying on his bed. I kiss the picture and put it under my pillow. It'll be nice to have an old friend close by.

Chapter 8

A Cold-Blooded Surgery

THE NEXT WEEK, Iggy the iguana is back. When I see her sitting rather regally in her owner's lap, I am proud to say I don't feel the slightest bit of apprehension. I feel better knowing that there isn't an animal Fitz hasn't dropped. In fact, I actually feel a certain fondness for Ike and Iggy and go right up to them.

"Hi, Ike," I say. "How's Iggy?"

"Doing okay but still no eggs, so I think we'll do the spay after all."

Dr. Fitzgerald walks out of one of the exam rooms and spots us talking. "Ready for your first surgery, Megan? I hope you don't mind, Ike, but Megan's going to do this one. I'm a little booked, and seeing as she has already put in two weeks at the hospital, I think she's ready for a little egg removal."

Ike plays right along with it. "That would be just fine. In fact, why don't I come in to stitch her up?"

At that, we all break up. Then Fitz says, "Seriously, Ike, we'll take good care of your baby. She should be good to go by tomorrow afternoon. We'll call you after surgery just to let you know."

"Shouldn't I be doing the calling?" I joke.

Fitz and Ike laugh. Then Fitz asks me to bring Iggy back to ICU so we can start to prep her for surgery.

"Have Terry help you with the lights. We have to keep her warm," he says. "And don't drop her."

"Thanks for reminding me," I say with a smile.

One of the things I've learned through Iggy is the difference between warm- and cold-blooded animals. We humans are warm-blooded, which means that with exposure to any outdoor temperature, our bodies stay the same temperature—98.6 degrees. Because reptiles are cold-blooded animals, their body temperature shifts with the surrounding temperature. It's important to keep Iggy warm because she can't do it herself.

Ike hands Iggy to me and I put her very carefully into the glass cage she'll call home for the next two days. Ike reaches over one last time to pat her wrinkly head. "See you later, bud." I can see how much he loves this tiny di-

A Cold-Blooded Surgery

nosaur, and I have to admit that I'm even beginning to see the appeal of a reptile as a pet.

I stay with Iggy the whole morning. I take her to ICU and get her set up under the lights. Later I follow her to X-ray. Finally I watch Sue Ann prep her for anesthesia. Like any animal, Iggy has to be unconscious for surgery. Once she is asleep, she has to be intubated, which means a tube is placed down her throat and into her trachea. A machine called a ventilator is then attached to the tube and does the breathing for her during the surgery. Iggy has a smaller throat than most, so Sue Ann has a bit of a challenge getting her intubated.

I have a hard time watching this part of the process, but I figure the least I can do is stick by her, considering I almost killed her last week.

Up until now I've only watched an operation through a window or door. This time Fitz says I can actually go in, but suiting up is a whole ordeal in itself. First I have to put on a cap to keep all my hair in. There are two kinds of hats. One is a shower cap and the other looks more like a surgeon's cap, tied tight to the head with a string in the back. I opt for the surgeon's version. Then I have to cover my shoes with shower-cap things. Then I get into a gown. Terry assists me with this since it's hard to tie in the back.

Then I wash my hands. Scrub them, really, with a brush and antibacterial soap. I scrub all the way up my arm because this is what I've seen Uncle Bob and Dr. Petersen do. All of this is so I don't bring any dirt with me into the operating room. Fitz is already halfway through the procedure by the time I enter.

"You girls. Always taking your time getting ready."

I watch as Fitz removes the eggs. I'm surprised because they don't look that different from the eggs at the grocery store. A little smaller, maybe. There are more than twenty of them! "No wonder this baby was tired," Fitz says.

Her and me both. It's hard work mothering an iguana.

After surgery, another emergency comes in. In some ways, this one seems even worse than Roscoe. It happens at about 3:00 P.M., just when I'm beginning to sweep the front area. "Two interns and a stretcher to the front lobby," I hear over the loudspeaker. "Two interns and a stretcher to the front lobby."

"Oh, God," I hear Carole say. "We've got an H.B.C."

I look up and see a woman running in the front door. Behind her is a boy around my age. They are both crying.

"We just called," the woman tells Carole. "Our dog has been hit by a car. She's in my backseat."

A Cold-Blooded Surgery

In an instant, the interns have the dog on a stretcher. They whisk her past me before I can get a good look. I think it's a yellow Lab. Carole takes the mom and boy into Exam Room Five and closes the door. After a minute she comes out and heads toward Treatment. I follow.

"Her name's Rasta, and she's sixteen," Carole tells Dr. Knor. "The family is up front in Exam Room Five. They want to do whatever they can to save her."

"Sixteen?" Dr. Knor says. "That's an old Lab."

From across the room I can see that Rasta's gums are pale, almost white. She is shaking and her breathing is very shallow. I don't even have to ask—I know she's in shock. Uncle Bob works with Dr. Knor to try to stabilize the dog. I don't think I've ever seen them look so intense.

"This one's got air in her chest." Uncle Bob calls out. "We need a tap over here."

Janelle runs over to the cabinet and takes out a needle. She attaches a tube to the needle and then a syringe to the end of the tube. I watch as Dr. Knor carefully places the needle between Rasta's ribs. I've learned that in a lot of hit-by-car's the blow from the car causes air to get trapped in the chest cavity, making it difficult for the lungs to expand.

Within a few minutes, Rasta's breathing a little easier, but I can tell that Uncle Bob isn't holding out a lot of hope. "This girl's old," he says over and over. "With a young one this would be trouble, but at her age, I can't imagine how she'll fight this."

Uncle Bob talks with Holly and together they head up to Exam Room Five, where the mom and boy wait for news. "We need to talk," I hear Uncle Bob say as he closes the door. "Rasta's a pretty old gal."

Soon the door opens, and the boy comes out. He goes over to sit in one of the orange waiting-room seats. He doesn't say anything, but he stares right at me.

"Hi," I say.

"Hi," he answers, then looks away.

I can only assume that his mom asked him to wait outside.

"I'm sorry about your dog," I say.

He doesn't look up. I understand, though. Sometimes if you're feeling overwhelmed or sad, it's hard to look into people's eyes. I decide to sit down next to him. I want to offer him a drink or ask him what grade he's in, but something tells me to be quiet. At least fifteen minutes go by and he and I just sit there, quietly staring. I feel a little awkward, but still I think I'm doing the right thing.

"Did you know that some bees have tongues that unroll until it's double the size of their bodies?" he says suddenly.

This seems like a strange first thing to say, but I have an answer immediately: "True or false—a snake can bite with its tail and its teeth."

"False."

"Very good," I say.

Just then the door of Exam Room Five opens. The two doctors and Rick's mom come out.

"Rick, how would you like to see Rasta?" Uncle Bob asks.

"I'd like that," Rick says quietly.

Rick's mom is Marissa. She puts her arm around Rick, and they shuffle down the hall. I can only imagine what they are feeling.

In ICU, Rasta is lying on the table. Her breathing is still pretty shallow, but steady. Uncle Bob takes a look at her gums, and Dr. Knor reports that her condition is the same.

"Definitely not worse, which is a good sign," she says.

Marissa starts crying again. Rick gets even quieter and looks toward the back wall. Uncle Bob and I stand back a little to let them have some time with Rasta.

"Marissa, we're going to do whatever we can for Rasta," Uncle Bob says. "Someone will be with her all night. And just like we talked about, we're going to get some X-rays and see what our options are. You are welcome to wait up front, or if you want to get Rick home, we can give you a call in about an hour."

After Rick and Marissa leave, Uncle Bob takes Rasta in to X-ray. I head to the kennels. I know that Bingo will cheer me up. I take him out of the cage and bring him out to the back patio. He starts to kiss me like crazy. I think he can tell I'm feeling sad. His efforts to cheer me up make me even sadder, and for the first time since I've been here, I cry. Big, fat tears that Bingo licks. "Bingo, stop," I say, but Bingo keeps licking.

"Bingo, no. Cut it out." Still he won't stop.

"Bingo, sit." I yell, and finally Bingo stops assaulting me. At the command "sit" he backs off and takes a seat.

"Good boy. You must have owners," I say, remembering how well he obeyed my commands last week. "What else can you do?" I ask him. "Can you speak?"

And then Bingo barks.

"How about roll over?" And he rolls.

I can hardly believe this. He knows almost every trick I can think of. Play dead. Give paw, go fetch. It's all there. Someone out there spent a lot of time with you, I think, as I grab his paws and ask him to dance. So where are they now?

By the time Uncle Bob finds me, I am feeling much better. But he seems a little down. Rasta's X-rays came

A Cold-Blooded Surgery

back. "Her lungs are clear, but her hip is shattered," he tells me, "so she's going to need surgery, and that's a bit of a problem."

Because Rasta is so old, surgery will be a risk. "That coupled with this recent trauma just might prove too much for her." He says Rasta's chest trauma will have to be stabilized before she can undergo surgery. "She'll be a guest in ICU for a while, I think."

Later that night I take some time to write to Sarah about Rasta—and Rick.

I really hope Rasta pulls through, but I wouldn't mind if she stayed around the hospital for a while, 'cause I'd like to see Rick again. He's one of the few people my age I've met here, and for a boy he's not that bad.

Chapter 9

The Queen of ICU

THE WHOLE NEXT WEEK IS A BLUR. It feels like I only go home to sleep. Dad says I'm a workaholic. "A chip off the old block," I tell him.

My official assignment for the week is to shadow Dr. Santen, the detective, but I spend every free minute in ICU with Rasta, who is making slow but steady progress.

Rick and Marissa visit daily. They come at lunchtime and then again right before dinner. On Monday, Rick spent a whole visit just lying next to Rasta on one of the mats. Since Rasta's hip is shattered, she's not in a cage. Instead she's on some transportable mats in the ICU, taking up half the floor. She wasn't interested in eating, but she did wag her tail a bit. She looked up from the mat when she saw the two of them coming in, and her tail unmistakably moved up and down.

"Hey, Mom," Rick said, "did you see that?"

"Yeah," Marissa said. "She still knows us."

It isn't until Wednesday that Rasta actually eats anything. Janelle and I feed her baby-food chicken off the end of a tongue-depressor stick—you know, the things the doctors use to press down your tongue to see if your throat is red. The way we get her to eat is really interesting. Janelle rubs some food onto the tip of her nose, in front of one of the nostrils.

"This way," Janelle tells me, "she's motivated to get it off. She should lick it off." Sure enough, it works. Janelle lets me put the food on Rasta's nostril and by the time Rick and Marissa show up for visiting hours that day I've given her a whole jar.

Marissa hugs me she is so happy, and Rick sort of taps me on the back of the shoulders. "Pretty cool," he says. I'm not sure if he's saying I am pretty cool, or if it is pretty cool that Rasta is eating. Either way, it doesn't matter to me. I'm just glad that Rasta is doing better.

On Wednesday afternoon an elderly woman brings in a ten-week-old Persian cat named Nibbles. The little kitten seems very tired.

"She was okay last night," her owner—a Mrs.

Knowles—tells Dr. Santen. "But today I can't seem to wake her."

Nibbles is curled up in a small blanket in Mrs. Knowles's arms. Though not totally asleep, she really looks out of it.

Dr. Santen asks me to get a weight on her, so I take the sleepy Persian from Mrs. Knowles and bring her out to the scale. She's so light she feels like paper in my hands. When I place her on the scale, I see why—she's less than two pounds.

Dr. Santen doesn't seem too concerned about the weight. He's more worried about her level of alertness. Her breathing seems a little slow, too. Usually a little kitten has a pretty fast heart and respiration rate.

"When was the last time she ate?" he asks.

"Let's see...." Mrs. Knowles is thinking. "She didn't eat at all yesterday, and maybe just a bit the day before."

Dr. Santen tells Mrs. Knowles that he'd like to keep Nibbles at the hospital for a few hours and put her on some intravenous fluids. Mrs. Knowles suddenly looks very worried.

"These little ones can't go too long without eating and drinking," he tells her. "But don't worry, they often bounce back pretty quickly."

After the IV is inserted, Nibbles goes into a small cage in ICU. "Keep an eye on her, will you?" Dr. Santen asks me.

"Sure thing." I think he can see how much I like her. Sometimes I think Dr. Santen's job is even harder than a surgeon's. He's the one who deals with pets who are chronically sick, or sick all the time. I think that would get depressing. I stay with her for the rest of the afternoon. It's amazing to see the sleepy kitten get more and more animated with each passing hour. By the time Rick and Marissa come in for their late-afternoon visit, Nibbles is back to normal.

"Who's that?" Rick asks after he visits with Rasta for a while.

"This is Nibbles," I say. "Want to hold her?"

Rick takes Nibbles, who is clearly not dehydrated anymore. Rick can hardly hold her.

"She's a squirmy little thing," he says.

"Yeah, now she is, but you should have seen her this morning."

Rick brings Nibbles over to see Rasta, who is also feeling much better. Rasta's head is up, and when she sniffs the little kitten, her tail wags so hard against the mat it sounds like thunder. "Are you going at it again?" Ray, the

X-ray technician, shouts affectionately at Rasta. "Rasta, you act way too happy for hanging around this place."

It's true. Rasta has been an incredible patient since the beginning. "She never complains," Uncle Bob had said earlier in the week.

"That's because she's royalty," Fitz said, patting her head. "She's a little queen."

And that's how Rasta got her nickname, "The Queen of ICU."

I can tell Rick and Marissa really like all the attention Rasta has been getting. I guess they feel less alone in this whole thing now that the entire hospital has fallen in love with their dog.

At the end of visiting hours, Uncle Bob tells Marissa that he thinks Rasta's ready for surgery. "As ready as she'll be, I think."

Marissa looks scared. "What if she doesn't make it?"

"Well," Uncle Bob says gently, "I hope she'll make it. She is an older dog, and there's always a chance that something could go wrong. But if we don't do it, she'll never get up. She'll never walk."

While Marissa and Uncle Bob talk, I ask Rick if he'd like to meet a friend of mine.

"Sure," he says, and we head for the kennels.

As soon as we step into the yellow room, Happy squawks so loudly that Rick jumps.

"Is this your friend?"

"No, that's Happy, and no one can make friends with her. She usually only talks to Janelle."

"Janelle, get out of town," Happy says.

"Or *about* Janelle," Rick observes.

We walk over to Bingo's cage, and as usual, he is delighted to see me. It is so nice to have someone be happy that you're around. "This is my friend Rick," I say to Bingo, and then turning toward Rick, "and this is my friend Bingo."

"Nice to meet you," says Rick.

"Likewise," a voice from behind the cage bellows.

"What was that?" Rick asks, smiling.

"That was Bingo," I say real serious. "Bingo talking through Matt."

Matt pops out from behind the kennels. "I love doing that," he says as he reaches out to shake Rick's hand. "Like I said, nice to meet you, Rick."

"Matt, Rick is Rasta's owner."

"Oh, Rasta," Matt says fondly. "She's a great dog. A great dog."

Rick and I take Bingo out to the patio so I can show

him all of Bingo's tricks. The one he likes the most is "play dead." Bingo rolls into a ball and doesn't move a muscle.

"Watch this," I say. I dance around and scream like a lunatic.

"That's amazing," Rick says. "He didn't even blink."

Then I tell him that no one has claimed Bingo and soon he will have been here for thirty days. "That's usually the cutoff for how long a stray can stay here before getting sent to the pound."

"I wish I could have him," Rick says.

"Me, too."

"Well, why don't you take him?"

"My dad doesn't want another dog," I tell him.

"Have you asked?"

"No."

"You've got to," Rick says. "Ask him tonight."

After dinner that night, I ask Aunt Barbara if I can use the upstairs phone. The extension is in her and Uncle Bob's bedroom, and I feel funny about going in there without asking.

"Of course," she says. "You don't even have to ask."

As soon as I hear Dad's voice, I know what the answer is going to be. He sounds tired. The plans for the museum he's working on aren't coming along as well as he'd like. "I think I might lose the bid," he says. "And I miss you, sweetie. Maybe that's why I'm cranky."

"Do you miss me enough to let me bring home the best dog in the world?"

He laughs. "Absolutely not. I don't miss you that much. And besides, how do you think Dixie would feel?"

I don't know. All I know is I can't let Bingo get sent to the pound.

Chapter 10

Breathing Easier

BY THE TIME UNCLE BOB AND I get in for rounds the next day, Rasta is already being prepped for her surgery. Sue Ann has intubated her and is shaving the hair from her hip. I feel bad because I wanted to see Rasta awake before she went under.

"How's the Queen of ICU?" I ask.

"She's doing just fine, Megan."

"Is there anything I can do?" I want to help with this dog more than any other I'd met so far.

"Why don't you help get her on the stretcher so we can get her to X-ray."

"Sure."

Right before an operation the doctors routinely get X-rays of the area they will be working on. They use it as reference during the surgery, and later, once the area is repaired, they compare the "before" X-ray with the "after" X-ray.

Rasta is like dead weight when we lift her onto the stretcher. It makes me a little sad to see her so out of it, so vulnerable. I just have to keep in mind that she's on her way to being able to walk again.

At seven-thirty, both Dr. Petersen and Uncle Bob are scrubbing up for surgery. Janelle has already given me permission to take off the morning so I can watch the surgery from the prep room, the same place where I folded towels with the interns not too many weeks ago. I set up a stool just below the picture window and right next to the phone. I told Rick and Marissa that I'd call to update them.

The surgery lasts about two hours. By the time it's over, I've talked to Rick six times. Rick asks me questions that, surprisingly, I can answer. The greatest concern with Rasta is the anesthesia. Even for the healthiest dog, there is an underlying risk with anesthesia—for Rasta, the risk is even greater. Her heart is not in its strongest state because of her age, and with the added trauma of the accident, her state is even more precarious.

"How's she breathing?" Rick asks.

"She's breathing fine."

I don't let on to Rick that I can tell Uncle Bob is a little tense. The surgery took longer than expected. "I didn't want to keep her under so long," he told Janelle about halfway through the procedure.

"I know," she said. "Hang in there."

I don't know if she was talking to Uncle Bob or Rasta, but her words scared me. I really care about Rasta—and about Marissa and Rick, too.

After surgery, Rasta goes back to her mats in ICU. Here two vet techs will monitor her to make sure she comes out of the anesthesia okay. I visit her periodically, hoping my face will be the first she sees when she wakes up. But even an hour after the surgery, she is still out cold.

Holly Knor asks me if I'd like to shadow her for a little while, to take my mind off Rasta. "I've got a case of the coughs," she says.

"Dogs cough?" I ask.

"This one does."

We walk into Exam Room Five, where a beautiful Beauvier is lying down on the floor. Beauviers are from France, and they are big and black—like an oversize Scottish terrier. This one is obviously tired. But even though she looks out of breath, her tail is moving a mile a minute.

"This must be Minnie Moo," Dr. Knor says.

Robert, the owner, tells us that Minnie Moo took sick after a recent stay on a farm. He said the dog had been doing fine for almost the full two weeks she had been there. "Then, on the last day, she started to act a little funny."

"Funny how?"

"Lethargic, I guess. Wouldn't eat, that sort of thing."

Holly examines the dog and tells the owner the same thing I've heard Dr. Fitzgerald tell his patients. The same thing I'll probably be telling mine in twenty years. "Since these guys can't speak, we have to figure out what's wrong through a process of elimination. The best way to do this is to run some tests. We'll start right now with blood tests and a chest X-ray."

Robert says, "Of course. Whatever it takes."

"And since her breathing is so labored, I think she needs to stay with us," Dr. Knor says. "At least overnight."

"Okay," Robert says. "Can I call later to see how she's doing?"

"Of course," Holly assures him. "Try not to worry. She's in good hands."

After Robert leaves, I ask Holly if she has any idea what's wrong with Minnie Moo.

"I think it could be a bacterial infection, or a fungus."

"Is it like pneumonia?" I ask. I had that once, and it was hard to breathe.

"Yeah, a pneumonia caused by a bacteria, which we could treat with antibiotics. The fungus is a little trickier."

"What's a fungus?"

"A fungus is an overgrowth of mold, like athlete's foot. Some fungi are difficult to treat. We'll just have to wait and see what the tests reveal. In the meantime, let's hope this gal keeps breathing okay."

But after lunch, things take a turn for the worse. Minnie Moo's breathing becomes so labored that the interns put her under a tent of moist air, hoping to loosen her cough. They also give her something called a coupage, which looks like they are beating on the side of the dog's chest. Holly tells me it's similar to burping a baby. "Only you're not hoping for a burp," she tells me. "You pat the area, and it loosens up the phlegm."

"It looks painful to me," I say.

"Well, it's probably not entirely comfortable, but the result is," Dr. Knor assures me. "She'll breathe easier."

Meanwhile, Rasta is still asleep. The operation was over three hours ago—that means her last dose of pain medication was administered even before that. Uncle Bob asks if I've checked in with the family recently, and I tell him I only kept in contact through the end of the operation. The last time I just told them I'd see them during visiting hours.

"Good. No need to worry them. This is something that can happen," he says, rubbing his face.

I can tell he's thinking again, and he's worried. This makes me a little worried. What if she doesn't wake up?

"Isn't there anything we can do?" I ask, more to myself than anyone else.

"What's her pulse ox, Terry?" Uncle Bob asks.

"Ninety-one percent."

"That's a little low. Let's get her on some oxygen. That might perk her up a bit."

Terry inserts a thin plastic orange tube into Rasta's nose and secures it to her snout with Krazy Glue.

"Is that really Krazy Glue?" I ask.

"It is, and it works great."

"Yeah, but how do you get it off?"

"A little Vaseline does the trick."

"Poor Rasta," I say in a baby voice. "Poor, poor Rasta." Then I kiss her on the nose just below the tube. When I lift my head, I notice her tail wagging ever so slightly.

"Did you see that?" I ask Terry.

"I sure did. Do it again."

"Poor Rasta," I say again, in the same tone of voice. The tip of her tail moves up and down.

"She's aware," Terry says. "That's a great sign."

"Everyone!" I call out. "Rasta just wagged her tail!"

After a half hour on the oxygen, Rasta is fully awake. It's a good thing, too, because visiting hours have started and Rick and his mom are on their way. I wait for them in the front lobby. I overhear Dr. Petersen tell Carole that Rasta is not out of the woods yet. "We'll keep her on oxygen overnight. That might help."

I ask Carole what Dr. Petersen meant when he said that Rasta wasn't out of the woods yet. "Well, Meg, she's an older dog. She might not make it."

My heart sinks when I hear this, but I see Marissa and Rick walking toward the front door, and I don't want them to feel worried, too.

Rick's mom looks like she hasn't slept in years. "Thanks for the calls, Megan."

"Yeah, Megan," Rick says, not meeting my eyes, "thanks." I can tell they've both been crying.

When Marissa sees Rasta, she starts to cry again.

"Rasta, my girl," Marissa says. The two of them lie down on either side of Rasta, hugging her. Since Rasta's been here, she's been kissed and petted by almost everyone on the staff. Last night I saw Uncle Bob get right down next to her and kiss her ears. I don't think this kind of affection would ever go over in a hospital for people. It would be too odd to have your doctor lie down with you and kiss your ears. Still, I wonder if maybe just a little bit more affection and connection might help people get better faster.

Rick interrupts these thoughts with a question. "What did your dad say?" he asks. "About Bingo."

I shake my head. "He said no."

"Darn," Rick says. Then: "Well, we'll think of something."

"We will?" I ask, surprised.

"Sure, we will, Megan," he says with authority. "We won't let him go to the pound."

Chapter 11

A Flight of Fancy

Dear Sarah:

How are you? I'm beat. There's so much going on at the hospital it's hard to know what to do next. I don't know how these vets do it every day. They have to take care of all these animals at once—and their owners. Like yesterday, Dr. Fitz had to calm down this lady with a sick turtle. Part of its shell was collapsing, and he fixed it with fiberglass!

We're all still worried about Rasta. But at least she pulled out of surgery okay. I think I may have helped give Uncle Bob the idea to try and wake her up. So I guess it's a good thing I came out here! I really hope she can go home soon.

When we get in the next morning, Uncle Bob takes Rasta off the mats. "Time to get up, girl," he says.

"Isn't this a little soon to have her stand?" I ask him. If it were me, I might just want another day of rest.

"No, Megan," he says. "She's been sitting long enough." He explains that all the time Rasta was getting strong for surgery, she was losing muscle strength. "We want to get her up immediately so the muscles around the bone are strong enough to support her. But don't worry, we'll give her a little help."

Uncle Bob places a towel under Rasta's belly. He gently lifts up both sides until she is standing with the towel supporting half of her weight.

"Megan, grab one side and let's see if we can walk her a little."

I take one side of the towel and together we traipse down the hallways of Alameda East with Rasta between us.

Everyone cheers. "Hail to the Queen of ICU," Carole says as we walk out to the reception area.

"The Queen's finally getting off her throne," Dr. Knor chimes in.

"Yeah," Uncle Bob says, smiling. "And it's about time. We need to get this girl home soon."

With Rasta up, the whole hospital seems a little lighter. All the rooms seem a happy yellow to me.

After we put Rasta back on her mats, I look around ICU for another patient.

"Where's Minnie Moo?" I ask Janelle.

"She's in Isolation," she tells me.

"Isolation" sounds so cold and lonely. "What's wrong with her?"

"Her results came back, and she does have a bacterial infection. Since it's contagious to the other animals, we put her in Isolation. You can go say hi. But make sure you suit up. We don't want her to catch anything else. Her immune system is suppressed."

I put on a gown, mask, and gloves to visit Minnie Moo. She looks better than she did yesterday. She has an IV drip going into her right paw. "Hi, Minnie, feeling better?"

For a minute, I expect Matt to answer, but then I remember I'm not in the kennels.

"I bet you are," I tell her. "Because whenever I have strep and I take the medicine, I feel better really quickly." Minnie Moo licks my glove through the cage.

At lunchtime I ask Uncle Bob if I can walk over to Birdy's house to see Goose.

"Rick's going to meet me there," I tell him.

"Oh, *really*?" he says in a kind of teasing voice, and

A Flight of Fancy

I'm sure my face is a thousand shades redder than the minute before.

It turns out that Rick lives exactly thirteen houses away from Birdy. I don't remember how it came up, but when I mentioned her name, of course he had heard of her. His mom even brought a bird to her once, before Rick was born. And Rick has always wanted to meet her.

Rick's bike is out front when I get there. He and Birdy are in the backyard, sitting around the patio table with a big pitcher of lemonade.

"Come on," Birdy says. "Have a glass of lemonade before we get started."

I can tell Birdy is fond of Rick right away, and he likes her, too. It's easy to see why.

"Do you know a bird's favorite color?" Rick asks her.

"Red, of course," she says.

"How do you know?" he asks.

"Because I know everything about birds."

I bet she does.

After we drink three glasses of lemonade each, Birdy asks us to get some birdseed from her garage. I feel like all that lemonade is swishing around in my stomach as I carry a big bag from the garage to the house.

"We'll start with the pigeons," she says. "Pigeons are very interesting creatures. Did you know that they are the most common bird in the world and that they are found in almost all cities?"

Rick and I follow Birdy into the screened-in porch, where hundreds of pigeons fly over our heads. Before we put out the food, Birdy asks us to wash the porch floor with special nontoxic cleansers.

"Watch out for your heads," Birdy warns us. "The one unfortunate thing about birds is they go to the bathroom just about anywhere."

"Great," Rick says sarcastically, but I can tell he doesn't really mind.

When we enter the living room, Edgar the raven screams "Never!" again. I wonder if that's all he knows how to say.

"Oh, he can say other things," Birdy tells me. "He can say 'Always,' he just won't. Edgar, won't you be good?"

"Never."

"Oh please, Edgar, won't you be good?"

"Never."

Rick and I laugh. Even though Edgar is saying only one word, this exchange between Birdy and the raven makes it seem like they have a real relationship.

Rick asks Birdy why Edgar isn't free.

"Edgar's wing is irreparable. If he were in the wild,

he would die. Some people think that would be for the best."

Birdy tells us that not everyone supports what she does. Some people feel that nature should select the survivors and that people who bring her birds are interfering with the natural order of life.

"Me?" she says. "I think I was born to do this, and you've got to do what you're supposed to do. Besides, I want all the little children who find a feathered friend fallen from the nest to have a place to bring it to."

Birdy has written a lot of books on birds. She publishes them herself. She pulls one out from a bookshelf in the bedroom, and on the back cover I see a photo of a much-younger-looking Birdy. A woman named Katherine who looks handsome and strong.

After we feed the pigeons and raven, Birdy tells us it's time to fly. At first I think she's telling us it's time to leave, but she means something else.

"Wouldn't you like to fly?" she asks us.

"Sure," I say. "Who wouldn't?"

"When I was your age, I went on a flight at least once a day," Birdy says.

"You mean on a plane?" Rick asks. He looks like he thinks she's lost it.

"A flight of fancy," she says. "It's easy."

Birdy tells us to close our eyes and imagine that we're growing wings. "Big, thick, white wings," she says. "Wings that will carry you over Denver, over California. These wings will get you home through any storm. They could carry your whole family and your best friend, too."

At first I feel kind of silly closing my eyes and spreading my arms out in front of Rick, but when I peek I see that he's doing it. It's one of those times when you want to burst out laughing, but Birdy is so serious that I know I can't.

Birdy tells us that now we've grown our wings, we need to open our eyes. "Birds aren't stupid. They don't fly with their eyes closed."

Then she leads us to her deck out back. It's really just a platform with a few steps leading up to it. There's no railing.

"Okay, you two, get ready to take off." Now I can see what she uses the deck for. She uses it to fly. "Okay? Ready, set, go."

Rick and I jump off the platform and hit the ground.

"Now flap," she says. "Flap around."

Now we can't help laughing. We three must look like lunatics, running and flapping and laughing so hard we can hardly see in front of us.

A Flight of Fancy

We laugh so hard we fall down. Then, suddenly, Birdy's laughter turns into coughing. It sounds like she's choking, and Rick and I get really scared and pat her back. In what seems like an hour but couldn't have been more than a few minutes, Birdy's fine.

"Happens from time to time," she says. "I guess I can't fly the way I used to."

When I get back to the hospital, I find out that we have a new emergency patient. A stray cat somehow found its way under a car's hood. When the car owner turned on his engine, the cat's leg got caught in the fan belt. The leg is so twisted that Uncle Bob doesn't think he can save it. The cat is already back in ICU, and I'm glad. I don't think I'll be able to look at this one.

The car owner, a man named Leonard, is beside himself. "I'll do anything," he says. "Whatever it takes. Just help the cat." Leonard feels awful that he almost killed the cat. "I'd adopt him myself," he tells Carole, "but I'm allergic to cats." He shows her his hands, which have already broken out in red bumps just from getting the cat out of the fan belt.

"Oh dear," Carole says. "I get that way with seafood."

Uncle Bob comes out and tells Leonard that they'll have to amputate the leg. Poor kitty.

"Then what'll happen to it?" asks Leonard.

"Well, we'll try to adopt him out," Uncle Bob says, "but it won't be easy. First of all, we have no history on him. This cat could be feral and could possibly have some health problems already. It's hard enough to place a healthy cat—now we are going to try to find a home for a three-legged one with questionable health."

"Oh God," Leonard says, "I can't just do nothing."

Leonard tells Uncle Bob that he's the kind of person who thinks everything happens because it was supposed to happen. He believes that each event is significant and he and the cat were brought together for a reason. "I can't sit back and do nothing."

Carole wholeheartedly agrees.

I think this is an admirable position to take, though I'm not so sure I agree. After all the hit-by-car's I've seen this summer, I do think some things just happen randomly.

On the way home that night, Uncle Bob and I talk about the stray cat's future.

"I know—I'll call Dad," I suggest. "He doesn't want another dog, but maybe he'll consider adopting a three-legged cat with questionable health."

"No way, Megan," Uncle Bob says, laughing. "No way."

Then I tell him about Birdy's cough. "It really scared me."

"Well, we'll stop by first thing tomorrow and check up on her, okay?"

"Okay." I know Birdy isn't lonely with all those birds to look after, but it makes me feel better to know that she has some human friends to look after *her.*

Chapter 12

Pig of Honor

TRUE TO HIS WORD, we get up extra early the next morning so we can visit Birdy before rounds. Uncle Bob's worried, too, that she might be sick. "Living with all those birds is a health hazard," he says.

"I think she *is* a bird," I say, "and she's immune to those germs."

"What an imagination you have, Megan," he says. "It's wonderful."

He thinks I'm kidding, but I'm not really. Rick would agree with me. And I think Sarah would see it, too. She'd know right away that an eagle or a sparrow or perhaps a bluebird was in our midst.

Birdy's house is dark, and I have to admit to feeling a little nervous as Uncle Bob rings the bell over and over. Even though I'm thoroughly convinced that Katherine

Hurlbutt is a bird, I have to remember that she is also eighty-six years old.

Then I notice that the bird taxi is gone. Sure enough, in another minute Birdy pulls into the driveway, a black crow in her net.

"Got an early call this morning," she tells us.

"Birdy, we just stopped by to see how you were doing," Uncle Bob says. "Megan mentioned that you had a little coughing fit, and I'd like you to see a doctor about that."

I take the crow out of the net, and just like Birdy showed me yesterday, I transfer him to the crows' cage in the backyard. I hear Uncle Bob tell Birdy that she might have some sort of bacterial infection. "It can be treated with antibiotics," he says.

"I'll make an appointment today, Dr. Taylor," Birdy says.

"I'm going to check back with you later this week, Birdy, so don't forget."

After rounds, Uncle Bob invites me on another trip to the zoo. He needs to check on the hyena. Pat has chewed at her bandage, and they want Uncle Bob to take a look at an X-ray to make sure the pin is still in place.

"Could Rick come?" I ask quietly. I don't want Uncle Bob to think too much of it.

"Sure, let's see if he's home."

"Oh, no," Marissa says when she sees us on her front step. "Did something happen to Rasta?"

"No, no," Uncle Bob assures her. "We're just here to see if Rick wants to come to the zoo with us. I have a patient there."

Color comes back into Marissa's face, and she smiles with relief. "Oh, of course. I'm sure he'd love to. Come on in, and I'll get him."

Rick's house looks a lot like Birdy's from the outside, but the inside couldn't be more different. Instead of a raven in the living room and a porch full of pigeons, there is a wonderful sunken den. This is how I always imagined a house in Colorado would look. A large, flowered couch and a coffee table made out of logs sit in front of a brick fireplace. The porch has log beams in the ceiling and two rocking chairs made out of sticks.

Rick asks me if I want to see his room. "I have some animals."

"Sure, I'd love to," I say. "Do we have time, Uncle Bob?"

"Go ahead—just make it quick." He stays downstairs to update Marissa on Rasta's condition.

Rick's room is cool. "Some animals" is an understatement. One wall is completely covered with pictures of animals—all different kinds. "Did you know that American black bears give birth to their young in the middle of hibernation? They wake up to have them. Then they go right back to sleep for a few months."

"That's pretty rude," I say, and we both laugh.

The zoo entrance is mobbed with kids when we get there. Every summer camp in the area must have picked today to visit. "Don't worry," I tell Rick. "We go in a different way."

At our entrance, Peter is waiting for us in the golf cart.

"Here to see Pat?" he asks Uncle Bob.

"Actually just to look at some X-rays and see the way she's walking," he says.

"Which do you want to do first?" Peter asks.

Uncle Bob turns to us. "What do you think, kids? X-rays, or the hyena habitat?"

"The real thing."

We pass the seal pool and the monkey house before reaching the hyenas. Uncle Bob hops out first and walks over to the edge of the habitat to observe how Pat is walking. The trouble is, the hyenas are in the same position they were in last time. They're all lying down on that same patch of brown grass.

"They're asleep again," I comment to Peter.

"I'm telling you," he says, "they all wake up when the zoo closes."

After fifteen minutes of waiting for Pat to move, Uncle Bob decides he'll have to come back another time. "Let me get a look at those X-rays now."

Pete's dad, Dr. Kenney, has the films on the light box when we arrive. "They look good to me, Bob," he says.

While the two of them talk, Peter and I show Rick the operating room and the cages. The hospital is empty now. "Everyone's pretty healthy at the moment," Peter says.

When I next see Uncle Bob, he has a big grin on his face. "Megan, you've been invited to a very special event. And you can bring a guest." He looks at Rick.

"Yes, Megan," Dr. Kenney chimes in. "We'd like you to come to our annual Do at the Zoo party."

"The Do at the Zoo?" Rick says excitedly. "I've heard that's incredible."

"And, Megan," Peter says, "you'll get to be at the zoo after it closes."

"You mean I'll get to see the hyenas awake for once? It's a miracle!" I say, and we all laugh.

Back at the hospital, I ask Fitz if it's okay for Rick to shadow him along with me.

"Sure thing," he says. "But first, Rick, tell me why a zebra has stripes."

Rick answers with no hesitation. "To confuse his predators. They can't tell if it's one zebra or many."

"Very good," Fitz says, and Rick beams.

"When it comes to animals, it's hard to stump this guy," I tell Fitz.

Fitz's next patient is a pig named Moo Shu who needs his nails clipped. This may not be as easy as it sounds—Moo Shu weighs more than two hundred pounds!

"Megan, why don't you get a temperature on Moo Shu?" Fitz asks. Just when I'm wondering why he would need a temperature reading for a grooming job, everyone in the room bursts out laughing. Since I know how an animal's temperature is taken—through the rear—I'm *very* glad Fitz was just kidding.

"One of these days we've got to get one of those ear thermometers," he says.

Moo Shu needs to look his best because, as it turns out, he is going to be the ring bearer in his owner's wedding.

"When is the wedding?" Fitz asks very seriously. Then he pauses. "Because this guy looks like a pig."

We all laugh. Moo Shu's owner, Diane, tells us she inherited the pig from an elderly neighbor. "I've never even had a dog, and now I own a pig," she says. "But I love him, and my fiancé loves him, too. We want him to be a part of our wedding."

I look at Rick and shrug. Different strokes for different folks, I guess.

"This is the neatest job," Rick says to me after Moo Shu leaves. "You are so lucky."

"She's not the only one who's lucky," Uncle Bob says as he walks up to Rick and me. "Rasta can go home today."

"That's great!" Rick says excitedly.

"I just called your mom, and she's on her way over."

Rick's big smile is contagious. I'm really happy that he can have his dog back. Another part of me is sad, though, because this means that Rick won't be around the hospital.

I think Uncle Bob senses how I'm feeling, because he turns to Rick and says, "Now, you'll need to bring her back twice a week for bandage changes. I'll give your mother all the specifics when she comes in, okay?" He roughs up Rick's hair.

"Okay," Rick says, still grinning.

Marissa shows up just before six. Uncle Bob is waiting for her. "This one's a fighter," he says to her. Uncle Bob gives Marissa all the post-op instructions and tells her to call if she has any questions. "She's still not totally out of the woods," he says. "At sixteen, Marissa, each day is a gift."

Marissa and Rick thank everybody for their kindness and hard work. It feels like a twenty-one-gun salute with everyone standing around watching. I don't think there is a dry eye in the place.

Rick stops me just before he gets into the car. "Thanks, Megan . . . for everything." Then he says in a whisper, "I think I've got a plan to save Bingo. We'll talk when Rasta's bandage gets changed."

I smile and step back as the car pulls out. There are at least ten of us out in the parking lot—Carole, Uncle Bob, Dr. Dan, Fitz, Holly, and assorted interns—waving good-bye. Farewell, Queen Rasta.

Chapter 13

A Case for a Detective

ON THE DRIVE TO WORK TODAY the sky was filled with angry-looking clouds. I should have taken that as a hint that today would be a day to remember. The second we walked into the hospital we were faced with another emergency. I've already had four so far, and I still have a little over a week left. Janelle was right—no matter how much we hope they don't, emergencies inevitably come up. I never would have predicted this one.

Four Scottish terriers—a mom and her three pups—lie twitching on the ICU floor, their eyes wiggling in their heads. "They're seizing," someone says.

A woman named Penny brought them in last night.

"It was like a nightmare," says Dr. Fitz, who had been on call overnight, "because she brought them in one at a time."

Apparently the mother Scottie, Tiff, started having the signs first.

"She came in unconscious and having seizures," Dr. Fitz tells Uncle Bob.

Then, a few hours later, the next pup came in. Then a bit later the next and the next. All with the same signs.

"It has to be some sort of poisoning," Uncle Bob says.

"You would think," Dr. Fitz agrees, "but the owner has scoured the yard and the house and has found nothing."

Uncle Bob decides one of the techs should take a ride out to the house to do a little detective work. "I'd like to know what we're dealing with," he says.

"Can I go?" I ask without even thinking.

"I guess that would be all right," Uncle Bob says. "Janelle, why don't you and Megan drive out and see if you can find anything. In the meantime, we need to get Poison Control involved."

Penny lives in a suburb of Denver called Crestmoor. It's very close to the hospital. From the outside, Penny's house looks ordinary—it reminds me of houses in my neighborhood in Santa Rosa. When we get inside, it's a different story. The place looks like a souvenir shop—chock-full of unmatched lawn furniture and plastic statues. There are also three different sheds to look through.

After three hours of searching, Janelle and I find nothing dangerous. Still, we're both convinced that there must be something in this yard.

The owner, Mrs. Fiest, is very nice. She feels terrible about what happened. "I'll never let them alone in the yard again," she says.

I want to suggest that she clean up a bit, get rid of all the junk, but then I remember what Fitz and I have talked about. A vet has to concentrate on treating animals with the greatest care and not judge the owners.

When we get back to the hospital, Dr. Stiecher, an outside neurologist, is examining the Scotties. He also thinks it's poisoning. "Either that or a very strange virus or bacterial infection."

But the Scotties aren't running a fever, and all their blood work came back normal.

"I can't imagine this is a virus or bacteria," Uncle Bob says. "But let's treat them for everything just in case."

Treating them for everything means putting them on an antibiotic to kill any bacteria, and also to keep them on fluids so if it's poisoning their kidneys and liver will be flushed out.

"The biggest problem with a poisoning is the damage it can do to the internal organs," Dr. Fitz tells me. "It's a wait-and-see kind of thing. We won't know for a while if their kidneys are damaged. We don't even know if they are going to come out of all these neurological signs."

The four Scotties now lie separately in the lower cages of ICU, still twitching uncontrollably. Each is hooked up to a separate IV. Except for the four Scotties, ICU is empty. The place seems strange without Rasta and Rick and Marissa.

I go back to the kennels to visit Bingo. He always makes me feel better.

"Hi, Happy," I say as I walk past the bird. "I'm Megan."

Squawk.

Bingo is up with his tail wagging as soon as he sees me, and I unlock his cage. When I put him down, I notice a black-and-white cat in the cage below. It's the one Leonard brought in. He's walking around on three legs as if he never had a fourth. "Hi," I say, reaching my hand into the cage. Janelle wouldn't approve, but the cat seems friendly enough. He comes up and sniffs my fingers.

Bingo and I turn to head out to the patio. As soon as I start walking away, the cat meows. I'd like to take him out, but I don't want to do anything that might mess up his bandage. I wouldn't want to cause him any more pain than he's already endured.

I'm still out on the patio with Bingo when Uncle Bob comes to get me. "Time to go home," he says, and he bends down to pet the dog.

"This is a pretty nice dog, huh, Uncle Bob?"

"Give it up, Megan."

On our way out the front door, we run into Rick and Marissa and Rasta.

I'm so happy to see them. I want to tell them right away how lonely ICU is without them, but when I see Marissa's face something tells me to be quiet.

"Rasta's not doing well, Dr. Taylor," Marissa says.

"Let me have a look at her," Uncle Bob says, and he and Marissa head off to Treatment.

"Is everything okay?" I ask Rick.

"I don't think so," Rick says, looking down at the floor.

"Want to meet a new friend?" I suggest, figuring I should try to get his mind off Rasta for a while. I lead him back to the kennels.

"Sure," he says not very convincingly. He kind of shuffles behind me.

"Watch out for Happy," I say. "She's a squawker."

"I know," he says. "I remember."

"Happy," I say, "you remember Rick?"

Squawk.

"I'm Megan, this is Rick," I say.

Squawk, again.

"I'm Megan, this is Rick."

"Janelle, get out of town," Happy finally says. I see a small smile on Rick's face.

"Come on," I say. "Meet our latest stray."

"Oh, what happened to him?" Rick asks when he sees the cat, who is now asleep.

I tell him the whole story about Leonard and the car engine.

"He's all alone in the world, just like Bingo."

"Speaking of Bingo," Rick says, like a lightbulb has gone off, "I never told you the plan. We'll kidnap him and hide him in my basement," he says. "Then, after I get my mom used to the idea, we can adopt him."

It sounds a little crazy to me. Steal Bingo from the hospital? "How could we do it without getting caught? There's always someone here."

"Leave that to me," he says mysteriously. "Don't wimp out on me, Megan. We can't let him go to the pound."

"I know, I know," I say, still worried. "But we're going to have to do it soon. Remember, I leave the day after the Do at the Zoo."

• • •

Marissa is sitting in one of the orange waiting-room chairs when Rick and I go back up front. She looks cried-out, empty. "Rick," she says gently, "remember what we talked about?"

"Yes," he says, almost in a whisper.

"I think we might be facing that decision," she tells him. "I think it might be time to let her go."

I want to scream, *Don't give up! Rasta belongs with you!* But then I see in Marissa's face a look of resolve, of peace. She has already made up her mind.

"Do we have to decide right now?" Rick asks her.

"Dr. Taylor is going to keep her on oxygen overnight. We'll have to decide by tomorrow, honey." She starts to cry. "We have to think about what's fair to her."

Rick looks a little shaky as the two of them get up and head toward the door.

"Good night, Megan. We'll see you in the morning," Marissa says.

"Good night," I say. "I'm sorry."

I walk back to ICU. Uncle Bob is shaking his head as he talks to Terry and Ray, who will be working overnight. "This was a tough one."

Rasta is once again on her mats. I feel sorry about

A Case for a Detective

what I wished before, that she could hang around the hospital longer. The Queen of ICU is so weak now.

For the first time I'm quiet on the way home with Uncle Bob. I look out the window at Pikes Peak, and I think about Rasta and Rick and Bingo and this whole crazy summer.

"How do you do it?" I ask Uncle Bob, finally breaking the silence. "How do you put a dog down?"

We talk for a long time about this part of being a vet. Uncle Bob tells me that he thinks putting a dog to sleep is a supreme act of friendship. "If the animal is suffering, it's better to stop the pain. I see it as a privilege sometimes, Megan, to be able to offer some relief."

I just wish it didn't have to be so hard on the owners and their friends, I think to myself.

Chapter 14

A Sad Privilege

RICK AND MARISSA are at the hospital when we arrive the next morning.

"We're going to euthanize her," Marissa says, staring straight through us.

Rick is looking down at the floor when he says very quietly, "Megan, could you be in there with us?"

I don't know what to do. I'm flattered that he wants me to be there for him, but I wasn't expecting to have to watch Rasta be put down. I feel too young, too inexperienced.

"You don't have to," Rick says when I don't answer right away.

"I want to," I blurt out.

"Are you sure?" Uncle Bob asks.

"Yes."

As we enter the exam room, a hundred thoughts race through my mind. Will I be able to watch? Could I ever do this to Dixie? Mostly I think of how brave Marissa and Rick are for thinking about Rasta's quality of life instead of themselves.

Uncle Bob explains what will happen. "I'll bring her in and give you a few minutes alone with her. Then I'll come back, and when you're ready, I'll inject her with a drug that will stop her heart. She won't feel a thing."

Rasta is brought in on a stretcher. "She can't even walk, Rick," Marissa says.

"I know," he says.

Uncle Bob leaves to get the shot. I turn around to give Rick and Marissa some privacy while they say good-bye. It's hard for me to swallow as the tears start coming.

Before I know it, Uncle Bob is back and asking, "Are you ready?"

Marissa says, "Yes."

Rick says, "Yes."

Rick strokes Rasta's side while Marissa holds her head. Rick breaks into sobs, saying, "Rasta, my buddy," over and over. I feel like I shouldn't be watching this. Then I remember what Uncle Bob said last night, about it being a privilege. I can see what he means, but it's a terribly sad privilege.

My legs are shaking, and even though I am standing in one spot, it feels as if I am moving. Whirling through space, looking down on a planet that will never be the same. Not without Rasta. Just then a ray of sun hits the window, and shafts of light come through the blinds. A wonderful orange light fills the room. Rick and Marissa look up at Uncle Bob. "It's okay," Marissa says. "It's okay now."

It's over—the whole miserable, wonderful ordeal. The four of us hug each other and say good-bye to Rasta one last time before we leave the room.

Rick asks his mom if he can stay at the hospital for a while. "Sure, honey," she says. "I'll come back and pick you up later."

"What do you want to do?" I ask him.

"Well, this might sound weird," he says, "but I'd like to go back to Birdy's."

Birdy is out back feeding the crows when we get there. "This one is ready to go," she says. She tells me it's the crow I put in the cage for her last week. I wouldn't have been able to tell it was him—they all look alike to me. Now his wing is healed, and he can fly away.

Rick tells Birdy about Rasta, and she gives him a hug.

"It's hard letting things go, isn't it?" she says. "I have to do it all the time, but it's always hard."

Rick and I watch Birdy take the crow to the platform we jumped off a few weeks ago. "One, two, three!" she says, and on "three" she thrusts both hands up to the sky and lets go. The crow moves slowly at first and looks almost as if it might fall. Then it figures out what it needs to do, flaps both wings, and is off, past the rooftops and past the trees. Up so high we can no longer see it.

Watching the crow fly away makes me breathe a little easier for some reason. I can tell Rick's feeling a little better by now, too. Coming here was good medicine.

The goose—the one that Fitz said was cooked—is happily walking around the yard in her makeshift wheelchair.

"Can you believe this?" Rick says laughing. "A bird in a wheelchair."

After this morning and after this whole summer, I can believe anything.

Birdy makes us lunch, and while we're eating I ask her, "Did you go to the doctor like you promised?"

"Yes, and make sure you tell your uncle that I did. He put me on some antibiotics, so I'm going to live, don't you worry. But I've got to get the birds out of the house," Birdy says calmly.

"What!" says Rick, almost spitting out his drink. "What are you going to do?"

"You mean, you have to let them all go?" I chime in.

"No, no, nothing like that," she says. "Edgar will go on the porch, and the rest of the birds ought to fit in the garage, or I'll just build some more cages out here. You're a strong boy, you can give me a hand."

Rick looks a little surprised, and then says, "You know, I'd like that."

"Good thing," I say, "because I don't think you have any choice."

We all laugh.

Just before I fall asleep that night, there's a knock on my door. It's Uncle Bob. "How you doing?" he asks.

"I'm okay."

"Hard day, huh?"

"Very."

"I have a little surprise."

He goes out, and a minute later he comes back and puts something black and white on my bed. It's the three-legged cat.

"What's he doing here?" I sit up so I can pet him.

"I'm going to adopt him."

"Really?" I smile so hard I think I might cry.

"Tommy and Allison wanted to name him Pizza, but I think Leonard might be better," he says. "I told them you get the final vote."

"Leonard," I say. "Definitely Leonard."

Pizza's ridiculous, I think to myself later as I try to fall asleep. I wonder if Uncle Bob would like to adopt a friend for Leonard. A certain dog I know . . .

Chapter 15

The Do at the Zoo

Dear Sarah:

You'll probably see me before you get this letter. It's my last Thursday night in Denver, the night of "The Do at the Zoo." Aunt Barbara insisted on washing my hair this afternoon, even though I told her I could do it by myself. She even set it in hot rollers. I'm still in them now, and when I look in the mirror, I see what can only be described as a freckled Martian.

Aunt Barbara bought me a new dress, a new pair of sandals, and—get this—lace underwear! I'm not used to having a mom fuss over me.

I'm supposed to be resting because Aunt Barbara and Uncle Bob have told me it's going to be a late night. I guess this "Do" is quite a party. I'm excited because 1) I'll finally find out what the animals do at the zoo when it's closed, and 2) (the real rea-

son) Rick will be there, too. He has this crazy plan to save Bingo, but I'll have to tell you about that in person.

Time to go—Aunt Barbara's here to take the rollers out. See you soon!

Love,
Megan

We get to the zoo at seven o'clock, just when the sun is starting to sink behind the cragged peaks of the Rockies. We enter through the main gate for a change, then walk with what seems like hundreds of dressed-up people to a big tent. I look around for Peter or the cart he drives so recklessly, but he and Dr. Kenney are nowhere in sight. Under the tent is a big buffet table and lots of smaller tables, each decorated with an ice sculpture. There must be at least thirty different sculptures here, each of an animal found at the zoo. There's a monkey, a polar bear, even a hyena. When I see the hyena sculpture, I tap Uncle Bob and ask where the bandage is. "The other Pat has it," he says with a laugh.

Rick and I get some food before the line gets too long. Then we decide to walk around the zoo to see all the animals after hours. First we go to the hyena habitat, and I'm thrilled to see that instead of lying around, they are awake and on the prowl. I don't see Pat, though. I hope she's okay. Next we stop at the giraffes. Hannah is outside, which is safe now that the sun is down. The giraffes stick their necks over the wall and peer down at us.

"Look," Rick says, "they know we're up to something."

The giraffes are right. On our way out of the giraffe house we run into Peter. He is driving the golf cart with an attachment that looks like a trailer. His dad and a few other guests are on board the trailer part, sitting on benches. "Hop on," Peter says.

Rick and I get up front with Peter and spend the next hour touring the zoo in the dark. Almost every animal is up and busy. The monkeys are cleaning each other. The bison are bathing. The only ones not doing much are the seals. That's okay, though. I've already seen them awake. As soon as Uncle Bob and Aunt Barbara signal us that it's time to leave, Rick and I get ready to put our plan into effect.

"Oh, no," Rick says when we're all in the car and pulling out of the zoo. "I left my bike at the hospital."

"That's okay," Uncle Bob says. "You can get it in the morning."

Rick tells Uncle Bob that he left it outside and he has put some important papers for his mom in the basket. "I

The Do at the Zoo   141

think I'd better get it, sir," Rick says. "I don't mind riding it home."

Rick sounds so honest and polite that it's hard for me to keep a straight face. But Uncle Bob doesn't go for it.

"Rick, it's almost midnight. You cannot ride home," Uncle Bob says. "I'll stop by the hospital, and you get the papers and put your bike inside overnight."

"Okay, sir," Rick says, and I wonder what we're going to do now.

Uncle Bob pulls up to the front of the hospital and puts the car in park with the motor still running.

"My bike's in the back, by the patio," Rick tells Uncle Bob.

"I'll go with him," I say, and jump out of the car before they can protest.

Rick gets his bike from the patio. I slip into the back door, to the kennels. Thank God no one is in there. With shaking hands I open Bingo's cage. He is so happy to see me. It's almost as if he's saying, "How nice to see you at midnight; I don't usually see you at midnight."

You're going to see Rick at midnight all the time, I think. I wrap Bingo in a towel and tell him to play dead. In order to get to the side door where I need to meet Rick, I have to walk through Treatment. I pile more towels on top of Bingo and carry him so it looks like I'm taking a bunch of laundry to the laundry room. My pile of towels can't bark, though. A barking pile of towels would be very suspicious.

Luckily, no one sees me, and Rick is waiting by the side door. Without a word, he takes Bingo and puts him in his bike basket. Then he rides toward the back of the hospital, to a path that will take him home. My job now is to stall. I take the pile of towels up to the laundry room. Then, very slowly, I start a load. I'm just about to pour in the detergent when Uncle Bob shows up.

"Why are you doing laundry at midnight?" he asks.

"I felt bad I didn't get it done today, and I thought while Rick was taking so long I'd come up here and do something useful."

He smiles and roughs up my hair in that way I hate and love at the same time.

"You're kooky," he says. "What are we going to do without you around here?"

Now I feel even worse about lying to him.

We go downstairs, and Uncle Bob tells me to wait in the car. "You must be exhausted," he says. "I'll go get Rick."

It takes Uncle Bob about ten minutes to realize that both Rick and the bike are gone. When he comes back to the car, he knows and he's mad.

"That's weird," I say. I'm so nervous my voice sounds squeaky. "He must be acting a little crazy because of Rasta and all."

Uncle Bob drives straight to Rick's house. I pray that Rick is already there. When we pull up, I see that Rick's bike is out on the lawn. Did he get Bingo past his mom?

Uncle Bob asks me to hop out and make sure Rick got in all right.

"Of course he did," Marissa says. "You guys just dropped him off, didn't you? I heard him come in. He went straight down to the basement."

"Okay," I say in my squeaky voice. "I just wanted to check."

I turn to leave, then stop. "And Marissa?"

"Yeah, hon?"

"Tell him to stop by the hospital tomorrow—it's my last day."

"I sure will," she says, and comes out and gives me a big hug.

Back in the car, I slump down in my seat. Our plan worked, but these grown-ups are experts at making me feel guilty. I can't believe it's 12:40 A.M. and I've got rounds in a few hours. My last rounds.

Chapter 16

Last Rounds

LESS THAN SIX HOURS LATER I'm woken up by Tommy's and Allison's voices outside my door. "Megan," they say, "let us in."

I tell them to go away and come back in ten minutes. The next thing I know they're in my bed—along with Leonard.

I dread going to the hospital this morning. I'm so tired—and worried. What will they think happened to Bingo? I'm also going to have to say good-bye to everyone today, and I know that's going to be hard.

"What's with the sunglasses?" Uncle Bob asks me on the ride over. "It's not very sunny today."

"Just felt like it, I guess," I mumble. I decided it might be easier if no one could see my eyes today.

• • •

Everything seems normal at rounds. I wonder if they even know Bingo is missing.

Then Uncle Bob says, "I have an announcement to make. Today is Megan's last day with us. She'll be going back home on Monday, after a weekend in the mountains."

"Well, I just want to say," Holly chimes in right away, "that Megan has been a great asset to the hospital this summer, and I am going to miss her."

"I agree," Steve Petersen says, and my heart skips a beat.

"Absolutely," Fitz says, giving me a wink.

"True," Janelle adds.

Their nice words barely register because I'm in so much suspense over Bingo.

Then Janelle says, "I think you should be a floater today. That way you can spend your last day with Bingo."

"Great," I say, a little awkwardly. Obviously no one has noticed yet.

I walk slowly into the kennels, wondering how I'm going to tell everybody that Bingo's gone. Matt is there cleaning out the cages.

"Bingo's out back on the patio," he says.

"He is?"

"Yeah, I put him out there this morning to entertain the others as I cleaned the kennels."

When I walk by Happy, I finally understand. "I'm Megan. This is Rick. I'm Megan. This is Rick," she says.

Shocked, I stare at Happy, then Matt. He shakes his head. "When I got in this morning, Happy was fluttering around her cage singing, 'I'm Megan, this is Rick.' I knew she was upset about something. Then I saw that Bingo was missing from his cage."

Matt called Uncle Bob right away, and they put two and two together. "It wasn't too hard to figure out. But I have to give you guys credit for trying," Matt says. "So anyway, after talking with your uncle Bob, Rick brought Bingo back. About a half hour ago."

"What?" I say. "Uncle Bob talked to Rick?"

I can't believe all this happened before we even left for the hospital. How embarrassing. Uncle Bob hadn't said a word about it in the car. This seems like something he would definitely mention. The fact that his niece went ahead and stole a dog from his hospital seems important enough to bring up.

"I'll be right back," I tell Matt, and I run upstairs to call Rick.

"What happened?" I ask him when he picks up the receiver.

"Well, I guess my plan failed a little."

"A little?" I say. "Though it wasn't totally our fault."

"Yeah, well, at least we know that bird is listening."

I have to laugh a little. Of all the times for Happy to start talking!

"Today's my last day," I remind him.

"I know. Mom and I are going to try to come up to say good-bye."

"You'd better hurry," I say. "I have the feeling I'm going to be fired pretty soon."

I decide to bite the bullet and go see Uncle Bob. I can't take the suspense any longer.

I find him in his office, doing some paperwork. He looks up.

"Why haven't you yelled at me?" I ask him.

"You know I don't yell, Megan," he says. "Besides, I understand why you did what you did."

"You do?"

"Sure. Why do you think I'm a vet, Megan?" he asks. "I love animals, too." Then he frowns a little. "But I am disappointed that you went behind our backs like that. Your plan was foolish, and Rick could have been hurt, riding his bike at midnight."

I start to cry. "I guess I just love Bingo so much, and I don't want him to go to the pound."

Uncle Bob lets me cry for a few minutes, then he says,

"It's okay, honey. I'll make sure Bingo gets a home. We won't let him go to the pound, I promise. I might have taken him myself, but now we've got Leonard."

"Why did you decide to take Leonard and not Bingo?" I ask.

"Bingo's a sure thing," he tells me. "Someone will adopt him, but a three-legged cat with questionable health? That one's not going to move."

I laugh a little and wipe off my face. "I feel so emotional today."

"You're tired. You had a busy night last night," says Uncle Bob, with a twinkle in his eye. "Why don't you go back to the kennels and take Bingo outside." Then he adds, "Just don't take him off the patio!"

The rest of the morning I spend running back and forth between the kennels and ICU. A part of me wants to spend all my time with Bingo, but everyone else is in ICU with the Scotties, who have made a remarkable comeback. Tiff stopped seizing last night and is alert. The pups have also stopped twitching, and their eyes are only wiggling a little. The three of them wobble around ICU, and it's hard to imagine anything cuter.

I ask Dr. Knor why it took so long for them to recover.

"We are lucky they recovered at all," she says. "Whatever these dogs consumed was some pretty powerful stuff." She explains to me that drugs and poisons have something called a half-life, which means the amount of time a particular drug stays active in your system.

"The more powerful the substance," she tells me, "the longer the half-life."

Holly and the rest of the staff have spent hours speculating about what caused the seizing in the first place. She and Fitz are convinced that it's strychnine, a poison that is still used in some gopher or rodent baits. "Maybe a neighbor was trying to kill some outdoor pests and a few pellets ended up over in the Scotties' yard," Holly says.

"Isn't it going to drive you crazy," I ask them, "not knowing for sure?"

"It's the nature of the job," Fitz tells me. "Remember, we work for silent patients."

Rick and his mom stop by in the afternoon. I can see that Marissa is feeling better.

"Mom says maybe we can take Bingo, Megan," he says, smiling.

My heart flutters a little I'm so happy.

"I just need a few more days to think about Rasta," Marissa tells me. "And Rick needs a few days doing extra chores to make up for that absolutely ridiculous plan . . . to steal a dog at midnight in the basket of a bicycle."

Rick and I promise to write each other. "Keep me up-to-date on Birdy, will you?"

"I sure will. And Megan," he says, suddenly serious, "thanks for being there through all this."

"You're welcome." I wish I could say it was nothing, but it wasn't. It was probably the most difficult thing I've done in my ten and half years on the planet.

When Rick and Marissa leave, I run upstairs to tell Uncle Bob that Marissa is willing to take Bingo. "Isn't that great news?"

"That is, though I think Janelle may have already found an alternative home."

"Another home?" I say, feeling sick to my stomach. "What could be better than Rick's?"

"Let's talk about it at home—Aunt Barbara has something special cooking."

The last thing I want to do now is eat anything.

Uncle Bob and I walk downstairs. "How about a final tour, Megan?" he asks.

We go through the same hallways and rooms we walked through just six weeks ago, but now everything seems so different.

In reception, I hug Carole. "I've got something for

you," she says. She gives me a framed picture of an eagle in flight. Underneath are the words *If you love something, let it go. If it is yours, it will come back to you. If it doesn't, it never was.* I start to cry, and Uncle Bob puts his arm around me.

In Treatment, I say good-bye to Holly, Fitz, and Dr. Santen. Fitz says, "True or false, Megan Taylor was the best intern Alameda East ever had."

"True," Dr. Petersen says, walking in from ICU.

"Definitely true," Dr. Dan says, arriving from Radiology.

Terry brings in a cake that says *Good-bye, Megan. We'll miss you.* We all eat it using depressor sticks as forks. I'm a little overwhelmed by the whole thing. My sunglasses are all steamed up.

I still have one more good-bye. The biggest one. I walk back to the yellow room, where Matt is cleaning out Happy's cage. "Good-bye, tattletale," I say to Happy. I walk by the two of them and head to Bingo's cage one last time.

It's empty.

"Is Bingo on the patio?" I ask.

"No," Matt says, looking kind of funny. "Janelle took Bingo."

My heart pounds. "Where did she take him?"

"She said she was taking him to his new home."

"What?"

I'm confused. Why wouldn't they have told me? They know what Bingo means to me. I run to Uncle Bob, who is waiting for me in the lobby. "Bingo's gone," I say, about to cry again.

"It's all right, Megan. We'll stop by and see the new owners, and you can see if you like them as well as Rick, okay?"

I calm down a little at hearing this, but a part of me is still very worried. What if the new owners are not so nice? What if Bingo ends up in an apartment and is cooped up in a crate all day, like Schatzie? My mind is churning with so many questions that I don't pay attention to where we're going. Before I know it, we're pulling into a driveway. A driveway that has become very familiar. Aunt Barbara, Allison, and Tommy are there holding a sign that says WEL MIS U, MEGAN.

"What about Bing—" But before I can finish my sentence, I see Dad standing off to the side of the garage. He's holding a leash with Bingo attached.

"Meet Bingo's new owner," Uncle Bob says.

I run out and hug Dad and then cover Bingo with a million kisses. "Is it true, Dad?" I ask. "Are we the new owners?"

"Absolutely," he says. "It's absolutely true. I just hope Dixie won't mind."

After a fabulous dinner, we all pile into Uncle Bob's other car, the Suburban. The sun is just beginning to go down behind Pikes Peak. After six weeks, I still haven't seen the mountains up close, so we are spending the weekend up in a town called Frisco. "It's about time we got you there," Aunt Barbara says.

Bingo sits in between Allison and me. Tommy keeps trying to climb over his sister so he can pet Bingo.

"I just want to make one stop before we head up," Uncle Bob says.

"Yeah, where is that?" Aunt Barbara asks knowingly.

I know the answer, too. "The hospital, of course," I say. "We've got to give Dad a tour. And who knows? Maybe Holly is working late tonight."

At this, Bingo barks.